"What Does A Man Look For In A Woman?"

Susanne asked.

"I don't know."

"Haven't women approached you?"

"No."

"Why not?"

"You don't look like you could be approached, and neither do I."

"I'm not so sure about that," Susanne told him. "I think, if I was a certain kind of woman, that I would approach you."

All his nerves danced. "Why?" His voice sounded strangled.

"Well, you look as if you'd be nice about it. And— you're very sweet."

"You can tell that just looking at me?" Cray asked.

"Oh, yes," Susanne told him without hesitation. "You just look like a very nice man."

Cray looked at her. She was walking along with her head down, watching the sidewalk. She was tired. He put his arm around her and supported her steps.

She laid her head against his shoulder. "I'm glad you're here."

Dear Reader,

Joan Hohl is back! And I know you're all cheering at her return. Her *Man of the Month* book, *Convenient Husband,* is Joan at her steamiest, and her hero, Jasper (also known as "Main") Chance, is a man to remember. That's *all* I'm going to tell you about this sexy, sensuous story.... You'll just have to read it for yourself.

A book by Lass Small is always a treat, and you'll all be thrilled to know that *A Restless Man* is the first in her three-book series about those Fabulous Brown Brothers. (Yes, you first met Bob Brown in her 1991 *Man of the Month* book, *'Twas the Night.*) Look for more of the Brown men in October and December.

August is completed with a terrific story from Mary Lynn Baxter, *And Baby Makes Perfect* (another hero to remember!); *Just Like Old Times* by Jennifer Greene (watch out for the matchmaking teenagers!); *Midsummer Madness* by Christine Rimmer (with Cody McIntyre, town hunk); and *Sarah and the Stranger* by Shawna Delacorte, a new author you'll hear more of.

Next month, look for Silhouette Desire books by some of your favorite authors, including Annette Broadrick, Diana Palmer and Helen R. Myers.

All the best,

Lucia Macro
Senior Editor

LASS SMALL
A RESTLESS MAN

SILHOUETTE *Desire*®

Published by Silhouette Books New York

America's Publisher of Contemporary Romance

SILHOUETTE BOOKS
300 East 42nd St., New York, N.Y. 10017

A RESTLESS MAN

ISBN: 0-373-05731-8

First Silhouette Books printing August 1992

Printed in the U.S.A.

LASS SMALL

finds living on this planet at this time a fascinating experience. People are amazing. She thinks that to be a teller of tales of people, places and things is absolutely marvelous.

One

"I don't think I've ever before heard of a couple marrying and then spending their honeymoon in the attic—at home."

That was simply a comment that Creighton Brown heard in the crowded living room of his parents' big, sprawling house in Temple, Ohio. Sitting back, relaxed, on the end of the sofa, Cray's eyes were closed. He tried to think who was speaking and couldn't identify the voice. That was because he'd been out of the country for so long.

Pretending to sleep, Cray could eavesdrop. He was tired of trying to explain himself, his restlessness, his adventures, the places where he'd been drifting in the world—

"It would be strange to honeymoon in the parents' attic that way."

Another voice added, "Rather embarrassing to anyone but Bob and Jo. They don't mind a bit."

A female voice said, "Well, the wedding was so unplanned. With only hours' notice, there wasn't any way to organize a honeymoon."

"They have the attic all to themselves. At least they don't have to share a room like some of us do."

"That's because there's so many of us. No one wants to stay anyplace else."

"That sounds so loving. You know good and well we're all afraid we'll miss hearing something if we aren't right here."

Cray listened to the gossip among his siblings, real and acquired. His brother Bob and Bob's new redheaded wife, Jo, were mooning around, completely unaware of the amusement they garnered. They weren't even aware all the others were gathered at the sprawling Brown house.

With his brother's wedding past, the New Year loomed, and Cray shivered in the unaccustomed cold. He felt a soft something fall onto his chest and opened his eyes. His dad had tossed him a sweater, and Cray smiled at his dad's retreating back and slid his arms into the sleeves.

As he positioned the cowl neck of the sweater, he could smell the comforting presence of his dad on the wool yarn. It was his dad's own sweater. Wearing it made the twenty-six-year-old Cray remember all the times his dad had done something just like giving a child his sweater to wear. It was a bonding comfort, to be wrapped not only in the sweater but to feel surrounded by his father's care.

For parents of their age, and of that time, they were long leaps ahead of most people in knowing how to nurture children. In a town such as Temple, they were very astute in the current thinking. Most of that kind of knowledge hadn't yet filtered into the countryside.

The town of Temple was just below Cleveland in northeastern Ohio. It was quite small and not on all the maps. It was on the southwest bend of the north-bound Cuyahoga River.

With Temple being that little, and a town that minded its own business and was therefore ignored, it had given his sister Georgia's Indiana suitor some problems when Luke lost her for a while. But Luke hadn't been easily discouraged and he'd hunted Georgia down.

Cray hadn't witnessed their wedding last summer. He'd still been in Australia at that time. He'd been on a walkabout. That was an Australian aborigine term he'd borrowed to explain his restlessness.

Now his brother Bob had married a Temple girl on that Christmas Eve. It had been an impulsive act, decided on after the Christmas gathering at the community center when everyone had gravitated to the Brown house. It was as if a plague of marrying was hitting the place. Fortunately, Cray didn't know any susceptible women.

And he'd been gone so long from home that he had lost contact with those he'd known. He looked at his last single brother, Tom, and his younger sister, Carol. They appeared to be secure in their bachelorhood. His other adopted and acquired siblings were a mixed batch. Some were married and some were not.

In a briefly peaceful moment, Cray lolled in the quagmire of visitors and relatives with assorted offspring and contemplated them with the distance of renewed observation. It was interesting to come back home after several years and look on his actual family and the adopted extensions with clear, detached regard. Varied as they were, they were a good bunch.

His parents, Salty and Felicia Brown, had been harboring stray kids all Cray's life. He'd never known a time that the house hadn't been filled. Right now there were six in residence, their ages six to sixteen. Cray smiled.

Growing up, there'd been so many kids around that no one had ever had the opportunity to be spoiled. Cray narrowed his eyes as he considered his parents. They were deceptively smart people. They were foolers.

His mother adopted the attitude of a spoiled theatrical devotee—blatant typecasting—and his father was a raspy-voiced ex-sailor. They were actually brilliant humanitarians.

What a shock to realize one's parents were superior people.

On cue, as was appropriate, his mother entered the room. She moved marvelously. Her throat was skillfully wrapped in silk, "to save her voice" for the play to be presented to the town in the doldrums of February.

That throat-pampering was a farce. Felicia was so fascinating that everyone waited to hear what she would say. So she wrapped her throat and allowed everyone else to speak, to tell her things, to confide, to confess.

Hidden by his dark, bushy beard, Cray smiled as he watched his mother. He knew that ploy. Felicia was a manipulator.

She came to him, and he was flattered to be chosen as her target. He wasn't even aware that he was flattered. He only smiled back and moved a bit to allow her to sit near him.

She sat down gracefully with a sigh. It was as if she'd done all the work needed for such a mob of people, when she'd done nothing but float around in her trailing gowns and mention what needed doing. Someone always leaped to amend any oversight.

She turned her big, dramatic eyes to her son Cray and smiled. He smiled back. She said, "I love your beard. How clever of you to grow it so perfectly."

His ego was stroked. "Men passing me on the street have said they'd grow one if they could get one like mine."

"Don't shave it off."

"I won't."

She studied him. "It needs to be trimmed—just a tad. Come. I have the perfect scissors."

And Cray stood up and gave her his hand to help her rise from the soft cushions.

As was usual, a number of relatives trailed along to watch, talking, commenting, laughing, sharing experiences and incidentally watching Felicia trim Cray's beard...perfectly. She only snipped minimally, it seemed, as she looked at him and smiled.

She hadn't allowed Cray a mirror, and a good indication of his trust was that he hadn't demanded one. It was she who said, "Would you okay it so far?"

His first reaction was, "I hadn't realized you'd cut so much."

And she said in her throaty whisper of a fake delicate throat, "Your beard makes you look like a young Errol Flynn, and with those straight, quizzical brows you seem amused by your disguise. You are a handsome man."

So he shouldn't have been surprised the next day when Felicia said, "I've had a letter from Susanne. Do you remember her?"

"Should I?" Cray asked.

"She's younger. Let me see. She is older than Peter, so she should be about...let me think...she must be about twenty?"

"How would I know?"

"She lived here for two years. Her family was torn apart by turmoil. You were at school most of the time. But you should remember her. She has gorgeous thick ash blond hair." Felicia sighed perfectly in assumed envy. "She was a handful." She had added that ruefully, then threw in, "A very obstinate child...very like Teller when he was first here last summer."

"What's she done? She in jail?"

"No." Felicia chided softly, with a slight smile that was so amused. "She's down in some town in Texas, living with an odd assortment of people."

"How...odd?" he asked with some caution.

"I'm not entirely sure." Felicia appeared to lose interest. Someone came along with a problem, a child needed to be held, and Felicia drifted away.

It was surprising how often Cray heard Susanne's name in those next several days. New Year's Day, after church and before the football games were to be monitored on four different TV sets, they all went back to the crowded house for a lavish dinner. It was Salty who raised a glass of wine and said, "To Susanne."

Felicia lifted her own glass and said in her soft, throaty voice, "To Susanne."

There'd been other toasts, solemn ones and hilarious ones, but Cray was conscious that there had been one specific one for Susanne, and that had been just her name. Nothing else had been added, no hope or wish or admonition to God to do something about her. That especially stuck in Cray's mind.

It was as if his parents had already discussed the entire problem with God so many times that He didn't need any reminders after the name identified the one. By then, God already had all the information He needed.

Cray wondered if, in his own wanderings over the past few years, his parents had drunk such toasts to just his name.

While that irritated him in some independent portion of his brain, his heart was warmed. He was reminded that he was loved. He was a part of people who were exasperated by him, who scolded him, who were impatient with him, who cared about him.

What a burden.

He was disgruntled. He looked around, at all the noisy bunch who claimed him as a part of them. He distanced himself. He was aloof. He was glad he didn't need the constant networking of humanity in order to feel his place in the world.

There were so many people who had nothing. How could this section of the population be so secure? They had food, shelter and warm clothing. Think of all the people in this world who had so much less.

And in his thoughts, Cray was critical of such security.

"Tell us about Australia," one encouraged in a friendly way.

He replied, "It's like being in a *National Geographic* spread."

"And the people?" the listeners encouraged.

"They talk in a different way. Some words are strange and corrupted to suit them. They are like all the rest of us."

"Would you like to live there?"

And Cray couldn't reply easily. "No. I don't think so."

"Why not?"

Cray shrugged. Why not? He avoided considering why he had returned home, back to this place. He'd only known that while he'd been fascinated by the people in other places, he'd returned to this one. If he'd had to come back, why was he still so restless?

The postholiday exodus commenced with calls and shouts, and wrestling packages and luggage and children into cars. Cray helped with the problems, but he had no sense of loss that they'd be out of the house. And he considered that.

He'd arrived unannounced while the town's Christmas caroling was in progress at the community center. He'd surprised them all. He'd apparently come home at this time to see them all. That was true. He faced that fact. Then why was he glad they were all leaving?

He didn't know. The critical restlessness that had driven him away from home was still festering.

After the house had been straightened, beds changed and the furniture replaced, Cray borrowed one of his father's used cars from the back lot at his automobile dealership. He did ask permission.

Salty's raspy voice said, "Use the yellow one."

"For cowardice?" Cray was snide.

Salty didn't appear to notice. "It has the best tires."

There's nothing worse than parents who are tactful without grinding it in.

So Cray went up to Cleveland and volunteered at a soup kitchen.

He didn't "see" the freeloaders who came well dressed and visiting together, taking enough food away for several more meals. He saw only the wretched ones, who were hollow-eyed and dirty. And he anguished.

He went home every night and silently disapproved of the hearty meals taken for granted. He quit eating meat.

He looked with some disapproval at his older brother Bob who, with Jo, was still living in the attic, taking his meals at the table with the others. Freeloading.

The weather turned, thawing the snows in a quirky couple of January days of milder weather. The river ran deep and the creek waters were rising, and people were volunteering with the sandbagging. Cray helped with that. Then, as the water rose higher, he went with a rescue crew, going into the houses and lifting furniture out of the water, rowing one of the boats to evacuate those trapped.

The weather changed again, getting colder and slowing the flood. Cray helped people clean their houses and get back into their homes. And he was impatient that they would live in the flood plain. Why didn't they move? The overwhelming flooding happened every six or ten years. It would happen again. And all the sandbagging and evacuating and harried work would be repeated.

Misery. It seemed to be everywhere, and he contrasted that to Christmas at home. All of those kinspeople had been clean and well fed, driving new cars from Salty's dealership.

He easily ignored or forgot how many of those kinspeople had been the children whose lives had been changed by his parents. He accepted that the six children who were living in that house had had no other place in the world.

He overlooked all the work and help that Bob and Jo gave to the family. Bob had taken over instructing the kids in chores outside and in how to handle tools. Jo supervised the housecleaning and instructed the six in the basics of household responsibilities.

Cray didn't notice. He discounted the fact that in order to help others, he'd had to search beyond Temple. No one in Temple needed help. Bob was employing a growing number of unemployed in his expanding billing-and-bookkeeping business, and he was beginning another business to assemble and mail catalogues. He was having to search beyond Temple for employees.

And each night Cray drove back home to Temple, filled the car's gas tank from Salty's pump and, after supper, he showered and put on pajamas and slept in a clean bed.

Salty finally mentioned, "You're freeloading here."

Cray replied, "I'm volunteering my time. People need help."

"I'm paying the gas for my car to transport you. You're living and eating here. You clean the barn."

That annoyed Cray. He was working his tail off— But he did recall his growing-up years and that everyone was supposed to pull his share of the load. He did clean the barn.

And Salty inspected it and sent him back to redo some of the work!

That really ticked Cray. His father was treating him like a child. So he was a little irritated and rough with the tools in his temper.

Twelve-year-old Teller came into the barn and stood watching. Then he said, "You should'a done it right the first time. Even I know that." And he left the barn.

That shocked Cray. He stood there not knowing how to vent his fury. But he began to remember other times his father had made him do things over. And Cray contemplated the fact that his father had been right. So had Teller. Cray looked at the sloppy work he'd done, and he redid it all more carefully.

At the soup kitchen the next day, he found that he looked at the people who came in wearing good clothing, laughing, visiting, carting off food for later, and he wondered why they weren't chopping food or garnering it, or cleaning the place. They were . . . freeloading.

Salty's rule that "you work for what you eat" had been ground in so long that Cray found his thinking was wavering. He became restless. For every really needy person at the soup kitchen, there were those who were taking advantage of the rule that no one was asked if he could afford to contribute to the pot.

So Cray asked some of the men—very casually— "Were you sandbagging during the flooding?"

And they replied, "My back's bad." Or they said, "I had to watch the kids while my woman worked." Or they said, "Nobody 'round us was flooded."

At the table that night, Cray complained about those answers.

The big boys listened. Teller especially. He studied Cray narrow-eyed and knowingly.

Bob and Jo didn't say a word.

It was Salty who replied, "People have to be taught to help others. Sometimes it's automatic. But most people don't realize what a difference they can make by just lending a hand."

Cray replied a little stridently, "No one told me to go help out."

Salty and Felicia never blinked an eye. They didn't even exchange a patient look.

Bob put his fork down deliberately and leaned back in his chair with some threat and looked at his younger brother.

Without lifting her glance from her plate, Jo cleared her throat.

Very sober-faced, Bob looked at his new wife, then picked up his fork and silently continued to eat.

At the soup kitchen, Cray became more observant. And he was more critical. But he also saw those who needed the help, who were incapable of helping others. The soup kitchen was needed by them.

He argued at the Brown table, "There has to be a way to solve this."

No one else interrupted or ever commented.

Cray was really arguing with himself. Salty and Felicia knew that and made sounds that indicated they heard him. Bob and Jo were silent. The kids ate and listened. They had been told to allow Cray his self-debate.

It was, by then, the end of January. Cray became progressively more restless. That was what had sent him off on his odyssey those several years ago. He hadn't gone off to expand his knowledge as much as he'd gone to—compare. To judge.

That was why he'd traveled so far physically. He'd gone on that journey, but he was back home.... Back to square one. He needed to decide what was important, what was not, and solve what he was to do about it.

The next morning, with everyone else gone from the table, Cray lolled in a restlessly lingering way. He was generally the first away, but now he sat there. He sighed to gain attention. It was Felicia and Salty's own son who did that, so it was well and dramatically a tired-soul sigh.

Although it wasn't breadmaking day, Salty just happened to be puttering around the kitchen, measuring the ingredients for bread dough.

Felicia was needlessly watering the potted herbs on the plank steps in the south windows of the enormous kitchen, and Salty had to go get the mop for the overflow. The plants hadn't needed watering. Cray didn't notice.

Felicia trailed over to the table and dropped like a damp handkerchief onto her chair to place a hand on her forehead.

On cue, Salty asked in his rasp, "What's the matter?"

In a deceptively lightened and pitiful sound, Felicia maneuvered her voice to be soul-tearing. "I'm worried about Susanne."

"What's she done now?" To focus Cray's attention, Salty paused and turned his body toward his wife, riveting attention on her wilting figure.

Marvelously controlling her basso profundo Talullah Bankhead voice, Felicia replied heart-wringingly, "I believe...she's in trouble."

"Pregnant?"

"No. I don't think so. But it's...some man."

They were really very skilled. They caught Cray's attention. He looked at his mother.

From the table she took a limp letter, which appeared to have been reread while weeping. Details are always important. She said in a trembling voice, "One of us should go down and see her."

"How can we do that? You've got rehearsals, and I can't let the kids live on pizza for the time it'd take for me to go."

"Mrs. Thomas—"

"She's got the flu." Salty said the lie with great concern for the healthy Mrs. Thomas.

Cray took the bait. "What's wrong with this Susanne?"

Felicia flared the dramatic eyes of a mother tiger. "'This'—Susanne?" She straightened and her nose hooked vertically like an eagle's beak, as her eyebrows did the same horizontally. It was stunning to see. "'This' Susanne is very precious to us. She lived here—"

"I know. You told me. For two years. I don't remember her. What's going on?"

"Some...man...is toying with her. I know this. I can feel it. I can see it between the lines of her letters."

With her remarkable facial alteration, Cray believed totally that Felicia could "feel" emotions from an absent child clear across the country—and he wondered if she'd known his restless unhappiness down in Australia. Had she?

His mother said, "I knew when you would come back. Your plane was early, but you delayed so that your entrance would be just perfect. You are my child."

He was stunned she'd know *that!* "I'm not that theatrical."

"Don't try to fool a fooler."

And Cray asked soberly, "Are you fooling me now?"

His parents' shock was so mild. A blink was all that altered their sober faces. They didn't reply.

Cray knew he'd offended them. He looked down and missed the quick glance between them.

Cray was serious as he glanced up at their blank faces. He volunteered, "I could go."

Then his parents exchanged the most marvelously innocent gladness over a problem solved. "Oh, Cray—" his mother said with emotion.

"Good." Salty's voice was approving.

"Where's she living?"

"Down in Texas." Salty supplied the direction.

"What's she doing there?"

"Working," Felicia fretted. "Off at the ends of the earth. No family anywhere around to help her."

"I'll go."

"Oh, I am so glad. She needs family around at this time."

"Okay." He was a little impatient. How could he be "family" when he didn't even remember this girl? "I said I'd go."

Felicia rose from the chair and walked over to Salty. With her back to her son, Felicia smiled her cat-with-the-canary-feather-smile, but her voice trembled with the perfect amount of relief. "He'll go. We don't have to worry now." And she leaned against her husband and lay her head on his chest.

Another flawless performance.

So Cray found himself packing, yet again, in order to move on somewhere else. That gave him a feeling of rootlessness.

Salty told him, "The yellow car's in good shape, you ought not to have any trouble. I got a navy buddy down there in the car business. Here's his card. If you have trouble, take the car to him. He can fix anything."

So could his father, Cray thought.

Salty added, "If you should need work, he might hire you, or he might have an idea where you could find work."

Cray took the card.

Felicia said, "One good thing about Susanne being in San Antonio is that your Australian clothes will be exactly right. You'll be comfortable there."

Salty rasped, "Why don't you keep my sweater. In the winter, even in Texas, there can be cool days."

Putting on the sweater, Cray mentioned, "You said a little town. San Antonio isn't little."

Felicia dismissed the deception. "They call everything 'little old' down 'yonder,' so I was just bracing you for that expression."

"Her last name's Taylor? And this is her address? Is the street on the map?"

"It isn't a long street, but it is at the corner of Fort Sam Houston, between it and the old thoroughfare of Broadway."

"Have you told her I'm coming down? What reason did you give?"

"We told her you're freezing up here in the north, in the snow, and that you need to be acclimatized before you try to live up here."

"I'm not sure I want to."

Salty shrugged. "You can live anywhere you want. Once you get accustomed to a place, it's the only place you want to live. I don't think I could stand good weather all year long."

Cray frowned at his parents. He knew he was delaying. He really didn't want to leave them again. He would do this favor, straighten out old Susanne, and come back home in the summer. That way, he could ease into next winter a little better. He looked out the window at the kids sledding on the hill behind the house. It wasn't a big hill, but then, with the slant, it wasn't a chore to tramp back up it. He remembered sledding that hill—

"How you doing on money?" Salty inquired.

"Fine. I've enough."

"You'll want to pay your share of the food." His father reminded him.

"I'll be okay."

"We hate for you to leave so soon," Felicia told her child. "We haven't seen you enough."

"I'll be back."

They hugged him with honest anguish and Felicia's tears were genuine because they annoyed her so.

Cray smiled.

He'd already said goodbye to the others. Bob was at his business and Jo was tutoring. They'd tactfully left him to say a private goodbye to his parents. Did his kin realize the wrench it was for him to leave? Apparently.

They went downstairs to the entrance hall and put on coats and boots. Bob had given Cray a ski jacket and knitted cap to wear.

The car was warmed and was standing, motor running, under the big, winter-bare elm whose branches covered the whole side yard.

As Cray put his suitcase and bag into the trunk, Salty whistled for the kids, and they and the dogs came running. The cats were in the window watching with interest.

Felicia was having trouble letting go of Cray and Salty blew his nose.

The kids were all pink-cheeked and laughing. They cheerfully yelled goodbye and waved.

Cray got into the car, put it into gear and eased off. It ran perfectly. He slowly drove away, glancing backward in the mirror. The kids had left. His parents stood there. His mother leaning against his father, his arms around her in support. She was weeping.

In the mirror they became tiny figures and still they didn't go inside.

Cray turned onto the plowed gravel road, and drove from the sight of them.

He was leaving ... again.

How many times had he left someplace? Home, school, towns, countries.

Pensively, he drove down through Ohio on the snow covered roads. He stopped and helped some woman get unstuck. She was suspicious and didn't leave her locked car. She watched him like a hawk. She was smart.

He stopped for the first night and slept heavily. Then he went across the bottom of Indiana and through St. Louis. In stages, he drove on down.

The weather changed as he left Oklahoma and crossed the Red River into Texas. It was perfect.

And he wondered what was the matter with Susanne Taylor who was an ash blonde and twenty years old. There was nothing exactly to pin it on—in the letters Felicia gave him to read. Susanne talked about somebody named Jack. Was she really having man trouble?

He narrowed his eyes at the road and speculated exactly why his parents had maneuvered him into this trip. He'd find out. He'd never been to San Antonio.

He wouldn't be wasting his time. He wanted to see all of the world.

He went through Austin, the country/blues music capital of the world. Then he came to New Braunfels, and finally he drove into San Antonio. He followed the signs to Broadway, went south toward the center of town and found the street exactly where it was supposed to be.

The houses were old. They'd had care and the neighborhood was settled. The house that was Susanne's was one-story, the yard was cared for and tidy.

Cray got out of the car in the pleasant coolness of early February. There were bare-limbed trees lining the street. He found himself wishing he still smoked. He wasn't entirely sure what to do next, and smoking would have delayed this next step. He looked around.

It was late afternoon. In the neighborhood, no one was outside. He wondered how many people were peeking around shades, wondering who he could be and why that tall, bearded man was there. Or maybe they all worked and no one was around at all.

Cray heard the house door open and looked up quickly. It had to be Susanne. At least she was at that house and her hair was ash blond. He watched her.

"Cray?"

"Where's the band? What kind of welcome is this? Do you know how far from Temple, Ohio, this town is?"

She laughed, and came off the porch and down the steps. "Oh, Cray, it is so good to see you again!"

She remembered him? How?

Two

Susanne ran lithely down the short walk, across the narrow terrace and flung herself against Cray. She hugged him just like they knew one another. She shocked him! And she was so soft.

His arms enclosed this stranger. He hugged her delicious body against his hungry one and was just amazed by how wonderful it felt. It was as if he'd never hugged a woman to him before that time. How could that be?

She released herself from his reluctant arms and glanced up into his serious blue eyes. She smiled as if that embrace had been an ordinary thing. Could she be that unknowing?

She asked in a perfectly normal voice, "How was the trip?"

Who cared? And he tried to think of a way to get her to hug him again. He said, "Salty and Felicia said to give you a kiss each." He did that. It took a while. She sputtered between the salutes and laughed. His voice a little thickened, he said, "Bob and Jo each—"

But she ducked away, laughing.

He complained, "I have to get them all paid off before I forget."

She blushed rosily and said, "We need to space them out."

Well, she had admitted she needed breathing space. She hadn't been that indifferent. Or—maybe she knew she ought not to encourage him! That thought sobered Cray. They *were* strangers. Then he considered perhaps the only reason she had said his name was because his parents had told her of his coming and had probably described the car.

He looked at the car. It used to be that a red car was noticeable, but now every other driver was in a red car. Yellow was different. This one was lemon yellow. In 1990, Crayola had discontinued their lemon/yellow crayon. That proved it was no longer a popular color.

Cray considered the car. The late afternoon sun was filtered through the bare tree limbs but it shone in shadowed patchwork on the lemon/yellow. The car was very noticeable.

The FBI probably had this car on its monitor. "That lemon/yellow car left from the Cleveland area and is now in San Anto—"

"Would you like some coffee?" Susanne asked with sparkling eyes laughing up at him. "A Coke soft drink?" she tempted. "Some beer. We do have some."

"We?" Had the letter mentioned the mysterious "man" had moved in? That raised Cray's hackles. For such a gentle, concerned, civilized man, it was startling to find he had primitive hackles.

"My housemates," she explained.

As he followed her to the house, the primitive man had to sort out the caring one. "You share the house?" She had been turning away, and he hadn't heard the plural S.

"It makes the rent reasonable."

They mounted the steps and crossed the porch. She opened the door and smiled up at him as she said, "Welcome."

He saw that her eyes were brown. He took the door from her hand and let her precede him. Then he followed her inside with quick glances for the "Jack" she'd labeled in her letters. No one else was in the small living or dining rooms. The rooms were so small that Cray felt a little claustrophobic.

The furniture was the blah type used in rental places. There was an anonymously brown studio couch with some jewel-colored throw pillows. Two easy chairs had been added to the limited space, and the inevitable coffee table was crowded into place. The TV was small, but they had a VCR. The floor was bare.

In the dining room were two card tables pushed together with a selection of chairs. A very nice china cupboard was packed with dishes of an odd assortment.

There was one wall of various-sized family pictures. He wondered if there was one of him. After he got his drink, he'd find an excuse to look. There were enough pictures that her share of the space could include all of the Browns' extended family.

There was a small hall off one side of the dining room, and across the hall was a half-opened door to a bathroom. Cray figured there were two bedrooms with the doors at either end of the small hall. He couldn't see into those two rooms.

They went straight on back into the kitchen. It was sparklingly neat and orderly. Susanne opened a jammed refrigerator and asked, "Coke soft drink? Beer?"

He had gone to the sink and was looking out of the window into a neat backyard with a small one-car garage. There was a vertical board fence surrounding the backyard. He turned toward and her asked, "Iced tea?"

She removed a tall pitcher already made up and poured him a glass. "Mint? Sugar? Lemon?"

"Mint."

They took glasses back into the living room and sat down. She smiled and said, "How nice to have you visit. How is everyone? What did you think of Teller? While you were gone, did the family letters catch up with you?"

"Now and then." And it was the first time he had known that the letters had been to all of the kids. Now, why had that surprised him? Hadn't he felt kinship with the unrelated kids? He looked at Susanne. He did not feel brotherly to her.

"You're just in time for our engagement announcement party."

His back shivered, and his mind went blank. "What?"

She repeated, "You're just in time for our engagement party. It's tonight. You'll meet Jack. He'll fit in with the rest of the family just perfectly. You'll like him."

Cray nodded in an unenthusiastic manner and thought, The hell I will. Aloud he asked, "Is he living here?"

"Of course not."

So her housemate must be female. That was comforting. "Have you known Jack long?"

"For almost six months." She said that with satisfaction.

Critically, he observed, "That isn't very long as a test for a lifetime commitment."

"We're very much in love. Wait until you meet Jack tonight."

"I'll look forward to the party. Is there anything I can do to help out? Do you need any errands run or punch stirred or tasted?"

She grinned. "It's all ready. I took off today to get it all done. And some of the people who are coming are bringing things, too."

"What did you 'take off' from?"

"I work for the city in the records-and-statistics department."

"Down in Australia I picked up an old *Texas Monthly* and read about the San Antonio cops."

"It's different now."

"Do you have a car? I didn't notice any cars on the street."

"I ride the bus. It's just two blocks to Broadway and the schedule is pretty accurate."

"While I'm here, you can use my car."

"I love the color."

She'd probably liked the lemon/yellow crayons, too. "What time's the party?"

"Well, the time's a little loose. We suggested seven o'clock, but Jack said he might be later than that."

"Could I shower here, if I mop up carefully afterward?"

"Oh," she blushed. "Of course. Do you have a place to stay?" She looked uncertain. "I'm sure you could sleep on the couch tonight, if you haven't found a place yet. How long will you be in San Antonio?"

"I'm not sure."

"Well—" She fluttered a little, undecided.

He couldn't give her an out. He had to be decisive. "Thank you for being so welcoming. And I appreciate the offer for tonight." With him there on the couch, Jack couldn't stay over very easily, on this announcement night. "I have a telephone credit card. May I call home and tell them I've arrived?"

"Oh, yes! And I'll get to say hello on your nickel." She laughed, so amused.

So the call was quite long. And at the end of it, Salty growled, "Look that guy over."

Cray replied, "Yes."

After the last telephone goodbye, Cray went out to the car and brought in an overnight bag from the trunk. He took the shower, put on clean clothes and mopped up the bathroom efficiently, thinking of Salty making him redo the barn. His dad would have had no complaints about the bath cleanup.

The housemate arrived home. She was female, dark-haired, young, attractive and welcoming.

So, Cray figured, each woman had a bedroom to herself. That was tidy.

Then another arrived, and another, and two more! Six? Naw, they were guests who'd come early. He felt crowded in that tiny house, with six such busy, charming women who chattered and welcomed him and talked at him and moved around getting ready for the party.

Cray thought it was very nice that Susanne had been in San Antonio long enough to have gathered that many good, easy friends. He found a place out of the traffic pattern, was handed a beer, and he listened and watched. It was quite a bit like home. Except that, there in San Antonio, the voices were all feminine, and at home the rooms were much larger.

He smiled at the six, watching, listening to them exchange the day's information, questioning, laughing. They were back and forth, into the bedrooms and kitchen. They set out food and a punch bowl. They tried to hang balloons from the light fixture, and Cray easily managed that for them. They gave exclamations of delight that he could.

Seven o'clock came and more people arrived. Male voices were added, and Cray was evaluated by the new arrivals and dismissed as no threat! That rankled. But others came and noted Cray and walked a little stiff-legged for a while. That soothed Cray as he helped them to accept him.

Quite a few of the mob were from the rabbit-warren apartment complex that covered a hill not far from their house. The noise level elevated and there was laughter. More couples came and the level of welcoming rose.

Cray watched as each male arrived, looking for Jack. He was reluctant to see Susanne welcoming Jack to her house. She'd been more than friendly, welcoming an unknown "brother." What would she do with a fiancé? Cray didn't want to see their greeting.

The party settled down. Food on the double card tables was replenished, more beverages were served. Toasts were drunk, and Jack hadn't arrived.

There were jostling comments—"Wonder if he'll make it to the church on time," and "Yeah, we ought to have a Jack delivery committee," and "Finding him at all might be the problem."

Feminine voices hushed the raucous predictions and the male voices laughed.

Susanne was discreetly anxious.

Cray heard several women speak in harsh whispers about Jack. "You'd think he'd at least show up tonight."

Cray asked, "Does he do this often?"

And they weren't sure how to reply to a stranger who represented Susanne's family. "Well, you don't yet know Jack. He's easily distracted."

"By... what?" Cray gave the woman a level look.

"Just about anything." Another woman said in disgust. "Have you met him at all?"

"No." Cray looked at her.

"Oh. Well. When you do, you'll see."

Cray sought Susanne and asked, "Do you want me to find him or call him?"

"No, he just about always gets here. Sometimes it takes a while."

"I'm not sure I approve of his conduct."

"Well, you're not the one marrying him."

"He won't change."

She blushed painfully.

Cray lowered his voice. "Are you pregnant?"

She was startled and her mouth opened and her blush vanished. "Of course not! We don't— We haven't— That's one reason he is— Well, it really isn't any of your concern."

"So you don't sleep with him?"

"No."

"Good."

"But after we're married, he won't feel so left out. We'll have each other."

"You mean he goes out with other women?" Cray was indignant.

"Well. You see, Cray, it's just that I don't believe..." She shook her head unable to explain.

"He's...punishing you?"

"After we're married, it'll be different."

"Don't count on it."

"Oh, Cray, you don't know him."

"I'm looking forward to...meeting him." But his tone wasn't very nice.

"I don't want you lecturing him. Do you hear me? Even if you are the only family I have here, I don't want you coming on with a heavy hand. It really isn't any of your business. You have to understand that."

"I'll behave as well as Salty would under these circumstances."

"No!"

"No?"

"Salty would 'bend' him. You know that."

Cray smiled with a gritty glint. That's all he needed to hear. Salty was very partial to all the kids, and he freely offered to "bend" anyone who wasn't doing right by them. Cray had forgotten that. What Salty could do, Cray could do. He quit drinking beer and went out of the people-packed little house onto the porch to breathe some fresh air.

After a time, Susanne came out on the porch and scolded, "I've been looking and looking for you. Why are you out here? Are you planning anything violent for Jack? You must not. I would be horrified and I'd be very angry with you."

"Don't worry about a thing."

"Cray, you—"

And a voice said out of the darkness, "Susanne? Can you all make a little less noise?"

"Weren't you invited? Who is it?"

"Mrs. Kennedy."

"Can you hear us clear over at your house?"

"Well, no. But I just happened to be walking by, and I heard some of the neighbors complaining, so I decided I'd better come warn you. They might call the police."

"Come have some punch. This is my announcement party. Jack and I are going to get married."

"Jack Terrill?"

"Yes. You remember him. You met him at—"

"I've been hearing about him from my kids. Why do you want to get tangled up with him?"

"Oh, Mrs. Kennedy—" Susanne wrung her hands and cast an anxious look up at Cray.

"And who are you? One of Jack's friends?"

Being one wasn't good, that was clear. Cray said, "No, Mrs. Kennedy. My name's Creighton Brown, and Susanne lived with my family for a while when she was a little child."

"I was eleven."

"Young." Cray gave her a grin on the dark porch.

"Where was that, where you lived?" Mrs. Kennedy questioned suspiciously.

"Up north in Temple, Ohio," Cray replied.

"A . . . Yankee?"

"Yes, ma'am."

"Hmm." That was Mrs. Kennedy's suspicious response. "What are you doing down here?"

"I'm going to bend Jack when he shows up."

Mrs. Kennedy took a quick breath and then said casually, "I believe I'll have that glass of punch—"

But Susanne didn't hear her. "Cray! You must not!"

"We'll see what excuse he has to be this late to an announcement party."

Mrs. Kennedy mentioned, "It's way past ten-thirty."

Cray recognized a bloodthirsty old lady. "Yeah."

Susanne went inside with Mrs. Kennedy to fetch the punch. And they'd barely wiggled their way inside the packed house, when one of the housemates came out onto the porch. Cray couldn't remember her name right away, and she didn't remind him of it.

She gave him a careful study in the little light cast through the cracked window shades, and she said, "You need to influence Susanne against marrying Jack. We've all tried. He's a flitter."

"Flitter." Cray tasted the word.

"He flits from one flower to another."

"Somehow I'm not surprised."

"How'd you figure that out?"

"No one is worried that he could have been creamed in a car wreck or hit by a bus. No one is surprised he's late on this special occasion. He's been late before."

"Yes."

"Can't any of you influence Susanne?"

"No. And it isn't because we haven't tried." She turned her back on Cray and looked restlessly out on the night. She turned to Cray. "He will leave. He is incapable of not tasting that next flower. You can see just by tonight what sort he is. Susanne doesn't need this grief."

"I'll do what I can." Cray looked off down the street and paced a step or two.

"Are you going to stay around?"

He contemplated that. "For a while."

"Susanne said you have dibs on the couch for tonight. It opens out."

"That'll help."

She studied him again. "You're a good man."

"I'm a restless, rootless man."

"Why don't you stick around for a while and be our adviser?"

"I just might." He gave her a sober, level look.

"Ah. This is going to be interesting."

"Maybe."

"You're going to interfere with Jack?"

"I'm going to bend him, if he makes Susanne unhappy."

"Well," she said cheerily. "This should be entertaining. I do hope he shows up. Can you whistle?"

"Very well."

"If I'm not out here when Jack shows up, please give me a whistle. I want to see this."

"I'll be a perfect gentleman until I need to take a hand."

"A primitive!" She clasped her hands together in delight.

"I am not!" He bristled.

And she bubbled laughter as she went back into the house.

It was a little after eleven, and Cray was pacing the driveway with unspent energy, when Susanne came outside. People had been out to smoke, to chat and to just breathe, the house was so crowded. They'd talked to Cray, and he had replied, but he'd been waiting. He scanned the short street. He was still waiting.

Susanne said, "Aren't you chilled? Don't you need to come inside? It's winter down here."

"This is Salty's Yankee woolen sweater. It's better than fur. Feel me." And his voice went a little husky between the two words.

She reached out an innocent hand and lay it on his chest. His breathing changed. She looked up at him with big, dark eyes and said, "Are you catching cold?"

He thought, I'll get sick and she'll take care of me. She'll sit by my bedside and put her hand on my forehead. She'll lean and kiss me to see if I have more fever.

How could she tell? He was hot for her. His body was heated and uncomfortable. He'd never felt such heat... Well, he'd never had this reaction to an unaware woman. He asked, "How many of you live here?"

"Six."

That did surprise him. In that little house? "Six? Five others?"

"Yes. It makes it so easy. We take turns with cooking and cleaning, and we have no trouble with the sharks. No sleep-overs, no pressure, no *room!*" She laughed.

"Sharks?"

"The predators. You get so's you recognize them."

What about Jack? Just from what little Cray knew of him, he was a shark. But Cray was going to sleep over. He considered Susanne. It was he who had the couch reserved. He asked, "Who is that dark-haired woman who lives here? The one who's a little older. Big eyes and great... uh... well built."

"That would be Sharon. We call her Shar. Why do you ask?"

He said, "She worries about you."

Susanne shrugged. "They don't like Jack. None of them. Jack says it's because other women like him."

"What about men? Do they like him?"

"He has friends."

"Regular men or party men?"

"Everybody parties."

"But do they ever meet for other reasons?"

"They work."

"Doing what?"

"Jack's a salesman. He's had wide experience. Cars, land, boats, advertising. He's very sharp."

"Maybe."

"Don't make up your mind about him until you meet him. He should be here any minute."

"You're too good for him."

"How like a brother to be prejudiced."

"I'm not your brother."

"Well . . . foster brother? You'd still be prejudiced. I lived in your house for two years."

How could he tell her that he didn't remember her? Cautiously, he asked, "When's the wedding?"

"Well, we haven't set an exact date as yet."

"Honey." His voice was gentle. "Have you pushed this announcement? Is Jack ready to get married?"

She stiffened. "It's his idea as much as mine. You're looking for something to make Jack look bad."

"Where is he?"

She almost lost her temper. "He *will* be here!" She flared her eyes at him and stormed off, going back into the house.

Cray felt bad that he'd pushed her so far. But she had to take another look at the guy. He was a zero.

And a car drew up to the curb in the line of cars parked along the street. It was a red convertible. Cray bet dollars to doughnuts that it was Jack. He slid his hands into his pockets and slouched a little as he watched a man get out of the driver's side. He went around the back of the car to the other side and opened the door. *A woman got out!*

Cray pulled his hands from his pockets in shock and stood up straight. It couldn't be Jack. With every spine hair bristling, Cray stood with his feet apart, his hand curled by his sides and his head a little forward as he watched the couple's approach from under his straight, quizzical eyebrows. He didn't look friendly.

He stalked down the porch steps and glared at the approaching couple. Then he made himself relax. It wouldn't be Jack. His own hostility was so high that he wanted the guy to foul up. No question of that.

Just being so late, as Jack was already, was foul-up enough. He wouldn't bring another woman to his announcement party... unless she was kin.

Looming in the darkness, Cray was formidable and the man's footsteps hesitated as he approached. The woman was unaware. The man said, "Are we very late?"

Cray replied, "It depends on who you are."

And the man said, "Uh-oh."

Very dangerously, Cray began, "Are you J—"

And some other people came out onto the porch rather noisily calling goodbyes. Their exodus swamped the three standing at the bottom of the steps.

Someone said, "Jack? Well, you did come after all! Congratulations." And another said snidely, "We've already given our commiserations to your future bride." And there was another comment. "What a jewel." The woman's voice was especially sarcastic.

Jack laughed.

Cray's exhaled breath should have set the hapless fool on fire. He asked the woman, "Are you kin to this nerd?"

She looked shocked and shook her head. "Good heavens, no! If I was related to him, I wouldn't have—"

But the screen door opened and Susanne called, "Jack? Are you here? I almost gave up on you."

"I'm here. I have a surprise for you."

Through his teeth, Cray warned. "You leave this woman outside. You tell Susanne when she's not in the midst of everyone else."

Jack gave Cray a dismissive look, turned back toward Susanne and opened his mouth. And Cray snarled, just to Jack, "Or I'll rip out your heart."

Jack closed his mouth and blinked at Cray. Then he quietly went up the stairs, abandoning the woman to Cray, and he never looked back.

The woman tucked back a strand of hair in a leisurely manner. She put her coat aside and smoothed her dress down her hip. Her breasts moved softly underneath the silken material. She was displaying herself. She didn't have on any underwear.

She smiled like a cat, as she told Cray, "You're really something. I've never seen Jack just walk away like that. He's a salesman, and he can talk anyone into anything he wants. I'm living proof of that!" And she laughed in a pleased way.

In a surprisingly soft voice, Cray asked her, "Did you know about the announcement party?"

"He told me it was a mistake. He's been trying to break off with her, but she won't take a hint."

"Are you the hint?"

That amused her. She told the dangerous man before her, "I guess you could say that."

"Go get in the car."

She agreed cheerfully. "Okay." And she gave Cray a big smile before she looked at the cars still on the street. "Which one's yours?"

Three

————

Coldly, Cray replied to the woman, "I'm not that easy."

But she grinned with delight. "I've never liked an easy man. I like to flirt and work a little. Let's get started."

"My mother told me never to take some other guy's woman home from a party."

"She's a cavewoman?"

"No. She a lady."

"No *wonder* I didn't recognize the symptoms."

The screen door opened and Jack came out from a silent house. He came down the steps to The Hint as he said, "Let's get out of here."

It was only then that Cray realized there wasn't a sound from the house. Where was Susanne? He went up the four steps in two strides and tore open the screen. The place wasn't as packed, but he still had to stretch to his height to see over and around heads.

No one said a word. The women were still, but the men shifted their feet a little. There was a cough. And in the dining room, someone cleared his throat.

Cray said quietly to those in front of him, "Where's Susanne?"

A man gestured, but a woman turned toward Cray and said quietly, soberly, "She went into the back bedroom."

Another woman told Cray, "She said to go on with the separation-announcement party, and she'd be back in a minute."

Wow. That was all Cray could think in his swelling pride in Susanne. She really had a good, strong spine, to give an exit line like that! She was hurting, and she needed him. He began to maneuver his way through the crowd.

As Cray worked his way toward that back bedroom, and Susanne, four of the housemates were saying, "You're not working well enough on the food. Each has to do his share. Do you realize the refrigerator won't hold all this?" And they were saying, "Put on Cray's tape by Bill Small's Heavy Weather. It'll start your cells moving." And they said, "Damn the torpedoes, full speed ahead!"

Cray hesitated. He couldn't go busting in on her with everything so under control. He couldn't move away, but he couldn't go knock on that door. Not with them all being so civilized.

And he realized for the first time in his life that he might not be civilized. The thought was distracting.

The music began. It was one of Small's blues tapes. The group began to ease up and to talk. In the severely limited space, some of them danced slowly to the music, adjusting to the beat.

Who could leave? Who could pull a long face? Who could do anything but help?

After a time, some of the men gathered at the little-nothing hallway and sang "Oh, Susannah!" facing the closed bedroom door. Talk about friends! And the chorus was "—oh, don't you cry for me—"

How old was that song? Even then, men were taking off and leaving women behind. Cray would never do anything like that. Well, there'd been that one woman in New Zealand. But he'd never said anything serious.... He wasn't like Jack. Jack was a bastard. And Susanne was hurting.

Cray couldn't push his way past the singers, so he had to wait. Then, with the song almost finished, Susanne opened the door. She lifted her chin. She smiled. Cray thought his chest might burst with compassion.

Someone gave her a glass, and she lifted it saying, "A toast!" People started hushing each other, and Susanne again called, "A toast!" One of the men lifted a chair over and another helped Susanne to stand on it. She smiled, with tears very close to the surface, and she said, "To the shortest engagement in this century!"

Everyone cheered ... Susanne.

Her glance quickly went over the crowd and found Cray, her stare clung to him. Her chin quivered, her smile returned brilliantly, and she inclined her head to him as she indicated her glass, then she drank it down.

Had Felicia been there, she would have been green with envy—before her own pride flooded in.

It was Cray who lifted Susanne down from the chair. It was he who was at her side for the rest of that night. It was his strong voice that began the short travel jokes, and it was he who encouraged others to tell their quick contributions of amusing close shaves and hilarious disasters. And it was he who saw to it that Susanne's glass was refilled repeatedly...with water.

The party became such fun for everyone else, that it was after three when the last one left. One of the trailers was Mrs. Kennedy.

Cray asked a couple to see Mrs. Kennedy home, and that cleared out the last of the stragglers.

The housemates busily, silently, cleared away what had to be done. Cray gathered paper plates and cups into a big plastic bag to be recycled. Knives, forks and spoons were put in a large pot of boiling soapy water to soak. And the five other women vanished.

Susanne got out sheets for the couch, carrying them to the living room.

Cray exclaimed, "Sheets? I wouldn't know how to sleep on...sheets!"

She almost smiled, but she put a finger to her lips for him to be quiet. Then she pointed to the bedrooms. He understood, and moved carefully.

Her eyes had circles of bruised blue. Her skin was pale and cold. He wrapped his arms around her and pulled her against his too-hot body and whispered, "It's the best thing that's ever happened to you. You may not recognize that right away, but it is true."

And she cried, her hand smothering her sobbing.

He picked her up and saw there was no rocking chair. He carried her quietly to a dining-room chair. He sat down on it, with her on his lap, and he teetered the chair back and forth on the back legs. It was a reckless thing to do. He figured if they fell over, the least it would do would be to distract her.

Quitely, he said, "Remember when Patty's husband left her?" Would she remember that? It had happened while Susanne was at the Brown house.

"He went back," she sobbed.

"But he had something going for him, and you have to remember that Patty was a harridan."

She huffed silenced breaths and whispered, "Are you saying that I—"

"No, no, no." He barely mouthed the sounds. "I'm saying that if there was anything honest in...that guy, it wouldn't have come to this. How can you be interested in a fool who would bring another woman to his anno—"

"He did *what?*" Her words were at normal volume.

Good God! He'd forgotten that woman hadn't been inside. Susanne hadn't known about her.

In sibilant steam she demanded, "He brought a *woman* here?"

Maybe it was better if she knew that. "Yes."

She sat there on his lap and was silent, her eyes moving around, not really seeing anything, her head turning in little alert movements as her thoughts spun along.

He didn't know what to do. Should he comfort her, or scold her, or explain reluctant men to her? Or should he tell her exactly what kind of male Jack was? He was well named. He was very similar to a donkey.

His lap was getting too excited to hold her very much longer. He was sweating in the cool air. His breaths were disturbed and shallow. All his nerve endings were aware of her being close to him.

How could he mention his need, when she was a stranger to him? The only thing she felt was sisterly affection. And of course, there was the fact that she was grieving for another man. That might be a deterrent.

How could he be lustful about this innocent stranger? It had never happened before, in all his travels, in all his life. Why this one? Why Susanne?

He was going to have to get her off his lap before he embarrassed them both. She was such an innocent that she probably wouldn't even realize what she was sitting on. What a precious girl. Twenty years old.

That was two years older than Felicia had been when she married Salty. Twenty wasn't so young. He kissed Susanne's cold, damp cheek. Her tears were for another man . . . or maybe just disappointment?

She could be disappointed. It would be a blow to find your late-arriving intended wasn't interested. He could have told her before the party. Jack knew she was having it. Everyone else was there. What a blow to her self-esteem to be told in front of everyone that she'd been wrong in her choice.

Then Cray thought what good friends she had. None had left. When Jack told Susanne, everyone there had stayed. They'd stayed and rallied 'round the flag. Cray thought kindly of them all.

Cray's lap wasn't distracted.

He cleared his throat and told Susanne very softly, "You need to take two aspirin and get some sleep. Emotions take over when your body's tired. Or would you like to go out for a walk? I could use some exercise."

That suggestion appealed to her. She shifted on his lap, about driving him crazy, and stood up. He had gone rigid and been unable to help her. She'd braced a hand on his chest and managed by herself. She was so distracted that she hadn't noticed his problem.

He insisted, "You need to get a jacket. And take your key."

"I'm fine." She mostly mouthed the words as she took her purse from a drawer in the dining-room china cabinet and removed her key, giving it to Cray. She continued quietly, "I could use the exercise, and I'll warm up soon enough. I can't go into the bedroom because I might waken Ellen or Sara. They are so sweet that they'll feel the need to get up and let me 'talk about it,' and I don't want to talk anymore."

"I've got another sweater in the car. It'll swallow you up." He looked down her and thoughtlessly added, "Take this one. It's Salty's."

"Oh." It was almost a silent keening. "I need it."

And Cray felt indignant. She didn't need Salty, she needed *him!* But then Cray remembered up at home how he'd felt when Salty had tossed the sweater to him during the holidays.

The two went out the door and down to his lemon/yellow car, shining even just sitting there in the dark.

Cray unlocked the car and lifted out another big, heavy northern sweater of knitted wool. He held

Salty's for her and Susanne slipped her arms into the long sleeves. It did, indeed, swallow her.

Cray lifted each of her arms and rolled the sleeves up so that her hands could be seen.

She folded her arms around herself and said, "Ah! It even smells like Salty. It's as if he's here with us. I remember when I was first at your house, and I must have cried twenty-four hours every day for a week."

Cray stared at her as he put on the other sweater. He remembered some kid crying like that. Felicia and Salty had been worried about the kid. One or the other of them had held her for that whole time. Then the cat had kittens, and the kid was distracted.

Aloud, he blurted, "Old Yellow had kittens."

"I remember! I'd forgotten that."

Hell, so had he.

Pensively, she shared, "Those two years were the greatest of my entire life."

Cray's eyes were squinted in the effort to help his brain remember other things about Susanne as a kid at his house. He drew a complete blank. But he *had* remembered that bit. Nothing significant. He'd been what, sixteen...seventeen? Those are pretty self-involved years.

They walked silently down to Broadway and then turned north. As they neared the entrance to Brackenridge Park, a police cruise car came alongside. The cop stopped and got out on the street side.

The pair watched with interest. Cray took another look around to see if anything threatened. Then he asked the cop, "Something up?"

"I'd have to ask you that."

"All's calm, as far as I know."

"She soliciting?"

Cray looked at Susanne, then back at the cop. "In that sweater?"

"She got anything on under that?"

"Now, now," chided Cray.

The cop said, "We've been clean around here for a while. We don't want them back along here."

"What?" Susanne turned and looked around, too.

"Doesn't she really understand?" asked the cop.

"Not her. She's clean. She had an upset, and we're just walking."

"You ought to go on home. The neighborhood association frowns on people walking around loose at odd hours."

It was irritating to Cray to be monitored. "It's a free country."

"Keep on and another cruiser might pick you up and let you explain to somebody downtown."

"You win."

"We do. Mostly."

"I'm on your side." Cray smiled.

"We need more guys to think that way."

"It must be boring, with it so quiet."

And the cop sighed. "It's what we want, but like you say, it's not lively."

"We'll go on back."

"See to it. I'll be around."

Cray nodded. "Good night."

The cop got into his car and slowly drove off. The couple turned their steps back toward her house.

"Did I hear right? Did he ask you if I had on anything under this sweater?"

"Yeah."

"Why, how rude!"

"Apparently, from what he said, they've had trouble with prostitutes along here."

She was a little huffy. "Not for over a year."

"You knew that?"

"It was in the papers, and the neighborhood association along here really got their backs up."

"You could have mentioned that."

"You... you would want..."

"Good God, Susanne." He was exasperated. "I would have known we shouldn't have been walking along here at this hour."

A little belligerent, she huffed an echo of his milder words, "It's a free country!"

"It's only free when the good guys rise up and see to it."

They were silent, walking. Then Susanne asked, "If you were walking along and saw me, would you... proposition me?"

He stared at her.

"Do I look like the kind of woman who would?"

"No." He thought of Jack's Hint. She sure as hell had.

"What... How... What does a man look...for...in such a woman?"

She shocked Cray. "I don't know."

"Haven't women approached you?"

"No." He said it firmly, as if it were the truth.

"Why not?"

"You don't look like you could be approached, and neither do I."

"I'm not so sure about that. I think, if I was such a woman, that I would approach you."

All his nerves danced. "Why?" His voice sounded strangled.

"Well, you look as if you'd be nice about it."

Oh, yes. Now what did he say? "You want to try me?"

"I wouldn't let Jack."

"You told me."

"But if I was one of the women along here, I'd want you."

He could hardly walk. "Why?"

"You're a very sweet man."

"And you can tell that just by looking at me?"

"You've been wonderful to me this whole day."

"And any prostitute, walking along the street, would be able to tell that about a man who would be willing to pay for her favors?"

"You look like a nice man."

He countered with logic. "You know my family."

"Yes. And I know you. You were just as nice to me when I lived with you all."

"Why did you leave us?"

"Don't you remember? Mother divorced that man and moved down here with her aunt. Then she asked Salty to bring me down here, and he did. We rode on the train, and it was such an adventure. After we got here, he stayed awhile to be sure everything was all right, and he needed to be sure I wanted to stay with my mother. That it was okay."

"I remember." He remembered the fact that Salty had been gone the night he'd broken the school's highest number of points in basketball. It had been that spring. It was probably the only time Felicia and Salty had been separated.

Thinking of Susanne, and how unsettled and abandoned she'd been, Cray realised how selfish he'd been at that time, and he finally forgave Salty for not being in the gym that night. What a selfish kid he'd been. He'd had no understanding at all for the other kids who'd been taken into the Brown household. He'd never really acknowledged their right to be there. It was like his being surprised the adopted and temporary kids got the family letters.

The realization that he'd been so unaccepting made his conscience squirm. And he'd considered himself a humanitarian?

He looked over at Susanne. She was walking along with her head down, watching the sidewalk. She was tired. He could see that. Perhaps she'd sleep. He put his arm around her and supported her steps.

She lay her head against his shoulder and allowed him to do that. "I'm glad you're here."

"I am, too."

"Why did you come down at this time?"

Ahh. How was he supposed to reply to that? The Truth Shall Set You Free. "Salty sent me to check out Jack."

She nodded against his shoulder. "He and Felicia would want to know. Have you called them?"

"Just that once when you talked, too."

"Let's wait a couple of days to call them again. Can you stick around?"

"I need to find a place to stay."

"No one else claims the studio couch. It's yours."

"One bathroom." He reminded her of that.

"There's a washhouse that was built onto the back of the garage. There's a washer and dryer. But there's a toilet out there and two big washtubs. There's a hot-water heater. That could be your bathroom and you could shower in ours during the day."

"It surprises me that you don't have basements down here."

"No need."

"Now, I've read that it can get cold down here. You do have ice storms."

"We did have one, and all the cars had a terrible time. People don't know how to drive on ice down here."

"Up in Ohio, they forget during the summer, and it always takes at least one nasty sleet storm to relearn."

"Do you mind driving on ice?"

"Not if the other car drivers, and especially the truck drivers, know what they're doing."

"Ah," she said on a shaky breath. "That's the way life should be. We ought not have to deal with people we don't understand."

His voice was gentle. "It would be very dull. You've heard the French salute, hooray for difference?"

"I think they meant sex."

"Not entirely. Women think differently, react differently, argue differently. You are a member of a very strange race."

"You have such a good, strong male voice. You did at seventeen."

"If I remember, that seventeen-year-old voice wasn't reliable. Sometimes it was adult and sometimes it was twelve." He looked down to see her slight smile.

They walked, then, in silence, until they reached her house. There was one small light on inside.

They went inside very quietly. She didn't offer to return the sweater. She turned and offered her mouth for his kiss so naturally that he had to restrain himself. She thought of him as "family," not as a male.

She then went limply into the back bedroom, silently opened and carefully closed the door. The house was completely quiet.

She must have just crawled into her bed in her clothes and that sweater? He hadn't been jealous of Salty in years.

He stood with his hands on his hips as he looked down at the studio couch which was lumpy, short and narrow. Disgruntled, he lay on it . . . and was instantly asleep.

The next morning was Saturday. Cray wakened and lay silently, taking a minute, trying to figure out where he was and in what country. He got up and sat on the couch in silence. The women were all still asleep? His watch said eight-forty-five.

He eased up and walked stocking-footed through the dining room, kitchen and gently unlocked the back door. He went out into the wonderful Texas "winter" freshness and prowled around the backyard, looking around. There were three cars in the driveway. They had to belong to the housemates, because there hadn't been any room for any friend to stay over.

The washhouse door opened at a touch to the knob, and the windows let in more than enough light.

He noted the half curtains and speculated if any of the housemates bathed in the big laundry tubs. He scanned outside the windows and saw that no house windows overlooked the back of the garage. It was private.

Everything worked well. The water had a good force. He went to his car, brought back his laundry and started a load. He washed at one tub and changed into fresh clothing taken from his suitcase. Then he went back to the house to fix coffee.

It was, by then, almost nine-thirty. The house was still silent. So was he.

He checked out the supply in the refrigerator and cupboards, and saw that lunch and supper were no problem. It was then that he knew he would pretend to be indigent, and he would stay there.

The house could use paint. So could the garage. One garage door sagged and was permanently open. It needed to be fixed. He would talk to their landlord and offer to paint and do repairs for two, maybe three months' rent. He would be helpful.

Salty had seen to it that all the kids were handy with tools. Cray carried his carpentry tools in the car trunk, with his tools for the car. It was a good way to pay someone back or to earn some money. He did good work.

The first one to stir from the bedrooms was Sharon. She came into the kitchen in a plaid wrapper and mumbled something as she poured herself a cup of coffee. She sat like a zombie and drank it. Cray said, "It's a great day."

Sharon ignored him.

He said, "Any chores open to be done?"

Sharon ignored him.

"You're a coffee addict and can't talk until the caffeine hits the bloodstream?"

Sharon ignored him.

"How many cups does it take?"

Sharon ignored him.

"Mexico has invaded the border to take back their citizens who've escaped over into Texas."

Sharon ignored him.

"Susanne is still sleeping?"

Sharon turned dead eyes to him and said, "Wogleious."

With some aesthetic enjoyment, Cray repeated with care, "Wogleious."

In an almost understandable manner, Sharon said, "Why don't you go for a walk?"

"Have another cup of coffee."

It took a while for the rest to crawl out of bed, and Cray felt almost at home. The only need was for some male voices.

Susanne was bravely moving around, still in Salty's sweater. A security blanket?

Cray said, "Sort your clothes, I'll handle the laundry."

No one objected.

He asked, "Any errands? I need to learn the town."

They made lists with directions.

Susanne was so pale that Cray made her "help" him. She had to ride along on the errands, so that he wouldn't get lost. Back at the house, she had to advise him if some garments could be washed with others.

She did respond ... but she wasn't alert. She would have to turn her head and consider. Then she'd soberly reply to whatever he'd asked.

The other housemates stuck around. They would just be there. They didn't demand conversation of Susanne. They didn't chat among themselves. They exchanged a lot of glances with one another. They were worried.

Cray put a glass of water in Susanne's hand every hour and a half and saw to it that she drank it. He coddled her an egg for lunch and he gave her soup for dinner. She was indifferent.

She was grieving.

Four

___

Sunday wasn't a very good day. Cray coaxed Susanne into going to a church. She had refused to face the congregation that knew her. She finally agreed to go to a small, unknown one.

Susanne showered and changed her slept-in clothing, but she was still wearing that sweater. She carelessly brushed back her hair and was "ready" without makeup.

Cray inspected her preparations, recombed her hair and tried to do her makeup. He was deliberately more inept than was reasonable.

Sharon, being the boldest of the six, was the first to almost volunteer her help, but Cray gave her such a hostile squint-eyed stare that she retreated.

He was so clumsy that finally Sara volunteered, "Here, let me."

And Cray said through his teeth, "Scat!"

Susanne finally roused enough to frown at him and then applied her own makeup. She wasn't carefully dressed, but who would notice...under that sweater?

Just the two of them went to the little church. Cray wore rather casual clothing in order to fit in with Susanne's attire. He greeted the preacher at the door and whispered, "Some man spurned her. What's your sermon?"

The preacher only briefly hesitated. "Forgive thine enemy?"

"No," Cray instructed. "'Stand up on your hind legs and howl.'"

So the preacher mentally dusted off an old Noah's Ark sermon about like being with like, shortening that part, and then expanding on how unlike *likes* can be. How we accept that we can be different from another person and not fit together. He did a really excellent job of it.

Going to church had been a try. Susanne sat in the church, but she didn't appear to listen. Cray had to help her remember to stand and put her hand on the hymn book so that it would appear that she was participating. He doubted that she was even aware of where they were, so Cray told God about this problem whose name was Susanne, and he did mention the rat labeled Jack.

When the service was over, Cray escorted his inert companion out and stopped to clasp the preacher's hand, leaving a folded twenty-dollar bill sticking to the preacher's palm.

Ellen and Agnes had fixed a very good dinner from the party dregs. The group had to finish up the meat.

The leftover party vegetables and fruits were a little tired, but the leftovers from those could be put into the compost pile in the corner of the little backyard.

Several of the housemates left during the afternoon, but Ellen and Sara stuck around, discreetly hovering.

Cray said, "Let's drive over into the park. The entrance isn't far. I've heard a lot about the zoo."

Ellen said, "It's very similar to this house. Odd assortments of creatures."

Right out of the blue, Susanne said, "But we fit."

Sara looked around the little house and agreed, "Almost."

However, Cray was electrified. Had Susanne been listening to the sermon? Maybe. If she'd caught that much, she might not be as zonked as he'd feared.

Cray went out to the shed at the back of the garage, emptied the dryer, put in another load from the washer, then filled the washer and started it.

The two alert women piled into the back of the lemon/yellow car. Cray eased Susanne into the passenger seat and buckled her seat belt. Then he got into the driver's seat and drove over to the zoo.

While the two women stood with Susanne, Cray got the tickets and they went through the gate. The zoo was an old one and had evolved into one that was well planned. They could have taken a trolley, but Cray thought the exercise would be good for Susanne.

So they walked, bought tidbits to throw to the animals, and watched the antics on monkey island. How charming to watch the monkeys. How delightful to watch the scamperings, the tumblings, the frolickings of all young creatures.

The children at the zoo were as wonderful to watch. The running, stretching-to-see, interested children were a show in themselves.

It was they who Susanne watched. Her face was moody. Her shoulders slumped.

They looked at a baboon. Cray said, "He reminds me of someone. Who can it be? I know. Jack!"

Instead of laughing, Ellen and Sara were so appalled that there was a dead silence.

Susanne said, "His lower lip isn't that pronounced."

Cray argued that, but inside his body he was exuberant. She might be okay after all. And soon. The sooner, the better.

They bought the inevitable hot dogs and iced drinks, and strolled around, eating. Susanne didn't finish hers. That was okay. She was eating enough for survival. And this was a form of survival. Her ego had been wounded.

Was her heart in shreds? That would be the test. If her heart was only bruised, she would be all right.

On their way home, Cray bought frozen peach yogurt as a treat, but the others weren't yet back. So the four sat in the dining room, watched the news on the little TV and ate the treat.

Then Cray went to a video store down on Broadway and rented an old Bud Abbott and Lou Costello movie. It was just right. Ellen and Sara were carried away by Cray's laughter, and Susanne did smile. She did watch.

When it came time for bed, Susanne's two roommates helped Susanne get ready for bed, reminding her to put on her pajamas and to brush her teeth.

Cray went out to the washhouse to remove the clothes in the dryer into the already loaded basket. He emptied the clothes from the washer into the dryer and put in another load of clothes to wash. He carried the completed loads into the house, and the two alert ones sorted through as to whose were which.

All busy routine.

Folded clothes were put on the owners' beds. Ellen put Susanne's away. Cray listened as the two cared for Susanne, and he wished to God that everyone who had been stunned by their emotions would have friends like those two.

The other three came in, not too late, and inquired, "How is she?" and "Is she all right?" and "How did you guys get along today?" and "Did anyone call for me?"

Cray replied, "Not bad." He said, "We went to the zoo." And he explained, "We weren't here. You ought to get an answering machine."

It had been a tiring day. His body was only a little tired, but the stress over worrying about Susanne had exhausted him. So Cray eyed that couch sourly again, lay down on it—and again slept immediately.

That Monday, five of the women were up in a practiced routine. They knew who was supposed to have the bathroom when, and they were quick and efficient. He told one who was dawdling, waiting her turn, "Why not use one of the tubs in the washhouse? It's a little like a Japanese hot tub."

And two of the women went out as if it were something of an adventure. Cray called after them, "Bring in the dry load, put the clothes from washer into the dryer and fill the washer with that last load."

One scoffed. "So *that's* why you had this bright
idea!"

And the other said, "Keep an eye on the bathhouse
door."

Cray grinned. "I'll come scrub your back?"

They said seriously, "We have strangers walking
through these streets. We don't use the bathhouse to
bathe, because we're alone here."

"I'll stand guard. Go ahead."

Those eating watched as Cray cooked and kept
watch out the window. And the back door was open.
They watched him as he moved, as he turned his head,
as he looked through the house to the front. He really
was on guard. He could handle anything that came
along.

One asked, "What should we do about Susanne?"

Cray replied, "I'll take care of her."

Quite seriously, Sharon said, "I'm glad you came
down from Ohio. Here's my office number, here in the
back of the book."

Cray glanced over and nodded. He looked out the
window, turned some pancakes, lifted others from the
grill, glanced out, stacked some on the plate and
poured out more batter.

The women smiled at each other. And the other two
said, "All our numbers are there. Sharon is closest,
since she works up at the burn hospital at Fort Sam.
But we could all come and help out if you need any of
us."

One said, "Susanne is lucky she has you."

Sharon mentioned casually, "I gelded Jack in my
sleep last night."

The women laughed. Cray looked out the window and saw the two scrubbed ones returning to the house. He met them at the door. "All okay?"

"That was fun!"

The nonparticipants asked, "Was there enough room?"

"The water's so deep that it's perfect!"

"I'm going to try that tomorrow!"

"Wait, you have dibs on the first shower."

"We'll have to set up a revolving schedule. Agnes, you're the scheduling genius."

She smiled in a sweetly fake way, "Agnes starts with an A so guess who gets first dibs tomorrow?"

"You have to move your car, Agnes, mine's second."

Cray offered, "I can do that."

"Thanks, Cray. Here're the keys."

They went out.

Of course, he had to adjust the seat, but he moved the car out and Trish backed her car free. She gave a wave and drove away.

Cray parked Agnes's car by the lemon/yellow car, pulled the seat up into place and went inside.

Sara said, "You're bright. You knew the next out was close to the garage. Me. See you guys for supper. Oh, hell, it's my turn to cook. You lucky dogs."

Cray said, "I'll have it ready. Don't strain yourself."

"A houseman. What a good idea. We'll keep him."

In an organized rush, all five were gone. Two had rides. The others picked up carpoolers along their way. They were all gone, the house was quiet, where was Susanne?

Cray tidied up the kitchen, did those dishes from breakfast and stood, drying his hand. He had to get Susanne up. If she stayed in bed all day, she would prowl all night. He would waken her. He went into the hall and tapped on the door. "Susanne?"

There was no reply.

He opened the door a slit and questioned again, "Susanne?"

She was silent.

Carefully, he opened the door fully. The room was jammed. Three single beds were so close together that the women would have to place their feet sideways to get between them. A pipe along the ceiling at the foot of the beds held a whole rack of clothing and under that burden of clothing were three chests of drawers. How could they sleep in that crowded room?

And his parents had felt bad because Susanne had no family around. That was really droll. No family? What she needed was some space!

He looked at his unknown foster relative. She was curled on her side and her hair was a tangle around her head. "Susanne?"

She made no move or sound.

Was she alive?

Cray pushed the middle bed over against the far bed and carefully moved along the minimally opened space.

She still didn't move.

He sat on the middle bed and reached over to brush her hair back.

She was watching him.

"Good morning, sunshine." His voice was husky and tender.

Without moving anything else, she blinked slowly and looked away sadly.

"Are you sick?"

She just looked forlorn.

"—or do you feel the need to grieve?"

She sighed. "Yes."

"Why?" He was really baffled, and his earnest voice reflected that honest question. Having asked if she felt the need to grieve, he then denied she could. "You can't grieve for that bastard. If you'd married him, he would have given you grief all your life. You have to admit that. Any guy wh—"

"Maybe if I'd been a little less— Maybe if I'd been a little friendlier—been more—familiar to—"

"No!" Cray's voice was harsh and dangerous. "You're not that stupid. Do you think for a minute that you were his first 'fiancée'?" Cray's pronunciation of the last word made the position sound as tentative as hers with Jack.

Cray stood up and moved out into the scant aisle at the bottom of the beds. He moved restlessly, trying to think of words Salty would have said to Susanne and couldn't think of even one. It was a little irritating to know his father had been able to advise and counsel on any occasion, and here his son couldn't deal with only one female.

Only one female? That attitude marked his time in Australia: the macho male considering the female the lesser species. It had been an easy attitude to absorb. He believed males not only dominated females but should keep them safe and in control. He was going to have to go back to tact. God hadn't given men any

other choice. That was probably punishment for
Adam lying about taking the apple first.

He glanced at the bed. She hadn't moved. Given his
own impulse, he would rip back the covers, swat her
backside and haul her out of there. She would get
mad, just watch.

Maybe a good, hot "mad" would be an
emotional physic. He went over and flipped back the
covers . . . there she was still wearing his sweater. She
was comforted by his scent, but she thought it was
Salty's. His scent had replaced Salty's. Cray tight-
ened his mouth and gave her a half swat. "Up and at
'em. Hit the deck. Let's get this show on the road."

She turned a dangerous glare at him and snarled,
"What do you think you're doing?"

"Prying you out of that bed." He was perfectly
logical and made his face look surprised that she'd had
to be told. "Come on. Up!"

She pulled the covers back up over her and settled
down with her back to him.

Obviously, he wasn't going to get her up too easily.
What a stubborn woman. That was probably why she
hadn't seen that poor Jack was not a willing subject
for marriage. She'd decided on marriage, therefore
Jack was supposed to have complied.

Cray said to the lump under the coverlet, "I'll give
you a half hour, then you will get up. Organize your
thoughts to doing that, or I will get you up and throw
you into the shower. Is that clear?"

He waited a couple of seconds, then stalked out of
the room in the silence. He didn't close the bedroom
door.

He went outside and got the last load out of the dryer and looked at the two deep tubs. They were set up on a sturdy rack, so that a woman scrubbing clothes wouldn't break her back doing it. Or a man. His mind added that since he was back in the States.

He folded the clothes in a pile and left them on top of the dryer. Then he went out into the yard. No man could grouse about mowing it, it was that small. The wire clotheslines were strung too low, and he felt no need to see how much he'd have to stoop to go under them.

He turned his head immediately and then looked up at the pitch of the house roof. There was room for an attic. He wondered if there was one. If he could move a sleeping bag up to the attic, it would solve most of his problems. He could keep track of Susanne and keep tabs on the neighborhood for the others.

Walking around the house, he saw there was a clouded little window at either end of the peaked roof.

He went back inside and began to look for access. There was a closet in the front bedroom, but no trapdoor. There was none in the hall or in the bathroom. Surely, as old as the house was, there had been a way to store things in that space in the attic. It was logical.

So he went back into the room where Susanne still lay silent and brooding.

He looked at the ceiling, then at the space behind the door. He pushed back the clothes that obscured his view and sure enough, there was a papered-over frame. A door? He went into the hallway and on into the dining room and kitchen, checking the depths of rooms, and went back to Susanne's bedroom.

"What are you doing?" The voice from the bed demanded impatiently.

"I think I've found a door to the attic."

She sat up. "A door?"

"Yeah." His tone was absentminded as he ran his hands along, under the ceiling-hanging clothes.

"Don't open it!"

Cray turned in surprise. "Why not?"

Big-eyed she said, "Skeletons."

He stared a minute, and then he said, "I believe I'm beginning to remember you."

"You didn't before?"

"Vaguely."

She became indignant. "Do you mean you came in here and kissed me and hugged me and slept on the couch, and you didn't *remember* me?"

"Felicia and Salty do." His tone was bracing.

"But you didn't?"

He hadn't. He still didn't. Not really. He explained, "I've been out of the country for a while."

"What's that got to do with whether or not your remember me?"

He turned away from her accusing eyes and reexamined the potential opening while he tried to think of a reply. He couldn't, so he asked, "Do you think the others would mind if we opened this up?"

"We?"

He looked at her in perfect logic and agreed, "You and I."

"How do I know you're really Creighton Brown?"

"Susanne..." He sighed, to show how patient he was being. "We called Salty and Felicia. You talked to them."

"You disguised your voice. They thought you were actually Creighton Brown. You became acquainted with him and studied his voice and learned about his family before you killed him in the Australian desert, took his papers and came here, escaping prison in Australia for murder. You grew the beard. His parents had never seen Cray in a beard, and they think under that beard is their son."

"I'm beginning to sympathize with Jack."

"You beast!"

With an irritated sigh, he turned back to the intriguingly papered-over frame as he advised, "Grow up." Then he went outside and looked for a ladder.

He found a reasonable one in the rafters of the garage. He pulled it from its nest, carried it over to the house and leaned it against the skirt of the roof. He climbed it cautiously, testing the ladder's rungs. They did hold.

He went over to the dirt-ground pane and wiped a reasonable circle of dust from the glass. In the faint cross light from the front attic window, it was clear that there was an attic, it was floored and he could just about stand up in it!

He went down the ladder and into the house. He ran into Susanne who was on her way into the kitchen. He steadied her and grinned. "There is an attic! Come look!"

"What's up there?"

"Goblins and ghosts."

"Cray—" She said it warningly.

"Come look, scaredy-cat."

"I was the only one in my troop who crossed the gully on a rope bridge."

He almost smiled. "That was very brave."

"I threw up halfway over. There was no way to get down, so I had to go on across. I was just as far from one side as I was from the other."

"That took more courage than someone who hadn't been afraid."

She looked down her nose at him and saw that he now had only one head after all. "I'll climb the ladder."

"Honey, if that's a problem, don't do it. I'll open the door behind the bedroom door."

"Why was it papered over? There must be some sinister reason."

"Why?"

She was annoyed. "Don't you ever read anything?"

"The Hidden Stair?"

"Yes! This is one of those!"

"Naw. There was probably somebody here with kids and they didn't want the kids up in the attic, so they sealed it off."

"The kids are up there? Their little skeletons?"

He drew in a deep, patient breath.

"Why don't you just break the window and look around inside first. You can tell me what you find, and it can't get into the house."

"Bats."

"Vampires."

"Susanne..."

"People like you get people like me into all sorts of terrible messes. You just go bullheadedly into things without thinking out the consequences."

"By golly, isn't that lecture fifteen from Salty?" Cray exclaimed.

"Oh, is it? I thought it was original from me."

"No," he said. "There's a familiar ring to it."

"Do you mean this isn't an impulsive thing, that you've been taking these sorts of chances all along? Why do you remember Salty's lectures so well that they are numbered?"

"You remember the exact words."

"Well, you see—" she faltered.

"What?"

"It's none of your business. I am opposed to your opening the door behind the door in my bedroom."

"We'll take a vote tonight."

"You aren't even paying rent!"

"I'll rent the attic. If any of you ladies gets tired of sleeping like sardines down here, you can . . . join me in the attic."

She gave him a careful look.

"Do you know that Bob and Jo spent their honeymoon in the attic at home, and when I left they were still using it?"

"Why?"

"Everybody was home and there wasn't any place for them to sleep together."

"Not everybody was there. I wasn't."

"Well, they decided on the spur-of-the-moment to get married. But you see, living in an attic must be genetic. My brother does, and it's natural that I do, too."

"I'm glad I'm not genetically kin to you all."

"You all? Honeychile, how long you been down in these here parts?"

"The expression included the whole Brown family."

"We all will see about opening up the attic when they all come home tonight, and then we will all take a vote. How will you all vote?"

"You all is never used for one person, so you must be asking how the housemates will vote. I don't know."

"Well, we have an exciting anticipation to experience until they all come on home here."

"Good grief."

He laughed at her and she did almost smile in response. He was pleased. He'd annoyed her enough that she wasn't a zombie any longer. "I have to go give Salty's greetings to a friend of his. Want to come along?"

"I think it would be wise to keep an eye on you. I'll call in to my office and make my excuses." She gave him a penetrating look. "A visiting 'relative' who needs direction."

He smiled like an amused satyr.

Salty's friend was called Pepper. Cray and even Susanne groaned.

"We was close as that." He crossed two fingers. "We was shipmates most of our trips out. He's a salt. Not just the name, but the salt of the earth. That saying has to be from when salt was scarce, before evaporation made the seas so salty. Do you know that in Roman times the men worked for salt? 'He isn't worth his salt.' That was a saying from that time. If he wasn't worth his salt, he hadn't done enough. See?"

"That's interesting." Cray smiled at the older man. "Have you and Salty been together at all since you gave up the sea?"

"I went up to New York last December when they were trying to get Bob and Jo to notice each other. We had a great time. Felicia is something."

"Yes." Cray and Susanne smiled at each other, sharing, and then they smiled at Pepper.

"Salt and Pepper." Susanne tried that combination of men.

"What one couldn't do, the other could. We was a great team. We could be depended on. Salty's the salt of the earth. I'm the seasoning."

The two young people looked at the old man and bet he'd been a handful when he was younger.

The old man said, "How about lending me a hand for a few days. I know you know about cars. Being Salty's son, you can do about anything. How about it? You can work here, look around and see what you want'a do."

"I'm obliged."

Pepper laughed. "Obliged? You got that one already? You're going to be assimilated."

"Assimilated? Now where did you get that one?"

"Salty. He kept telling me I oughta do that. If I did, I wouldn'ta spent so much time in the brig. Never did get assimilated. But I learned the word."

"I'd be proud to work with you."

"I pay regular wages. Come around in a couple of days. I'll have something lined up for you to take on."

"Thank you."

"And honey, if you'd like to sit on my lap and answer the phone, I'd appreciate it."

"No!" she laughed.

"I could grow on you." His eyes were wicked in his wrinkled smile.

"Watch it, Pepper." Cray's voice was deceptively mild.

"You got her branded?"

"Not yet."

And Susanne blinked. What did Cray mean by that?

Five

That night after supper, Cray brought up the matter of a possible attic door. There wasn't even a chance to take a vote. The collected five were astonished there could be a door to the attic. In a spontaneous exodus, they surged up from their chairs and went toward the bedroom.

There simply wasn't enough room for them all, and there was a people jam trying to get into the bedroom all at once and find a place to stand.

Cray's deep voice commanded their attention as he said, "Ladies, I know how to open that door. Let me do it."

"I have a nail file," one female voice volunteered.

And another replied, "I have a screwdriver! That'll do it. We just need to rip the paper."

"No!" Cray bellowed. "Cut it out! I know—"

"Cut it out? That's what we're trying to do!"

"Stop!" Cray changed his wordage. "Stand back and let me do it."

They really didn't want to give up being the first to actually see what was there.

"It could just be a ventilation shaft."

"Or a dead body...entombed."

"Susanne! Quit that!"

"Well, I've heard—"

Sara asked quickly, "What? What did you hear? Moaning?"

"Ladies! Will you stop this and let me through?"

"Oh, Cray, you're such a spoilsport."

"I don't want the owner suing us for damage. We have to cut this carefully. How do we know it will lead to the attic? If it does, and you have more room, he could up the rent."

"Oh, great." One voice was disgruntled.

He chided, "Now, you know you only pay fifty bucks apiece."

"We don't make enough to be stuck with more rent. Let's leave the thing blocked."

Agnes countered, "No, let's open it up."

"Vote!" Cray was exasperated.

The five do's won over two don'ts.

Cray lifted women aside, garnering all sorts of comments. But worse, the moved ones began shouldering the others aside so that he could repeat the liftings.

Susanne became hostile.

The others attributed the hostility to Susanne being outvoted in keeping the attic closed.

With a wicked kitchen knife, Cray carefully slit the paper along the inside of the jam. By doing it that way, it would be easier to conceal a faulty intrusion past the door if there was no reason to have it opened.

There were whispers of excitement. And women stood on the beds to get a better view as Cray worked very efficiently. The hinges were revealed, and it was obvious more than one covering of paper had been used. The attic had been sealed off for years.

The place for the knob was an empty hole. Cray put his fingers into the small opening and carefully pulled the door.

Creaking, making little noises of additional separations of paper, the door slowly began to swing open.

Cray was careful to avoid undue damage to the paper as he coaxed the door to swing wide.

And the room was silent. No one even breathed.

It was dark inside the entrance. It was a yawning opening of just black. They leaned to see, holding their breaths.

There wasn't a discernible skeleton. There were—stairs.

There were also gasps from the watchers.

"Who wants to go up?" Cray was being humorous. He thought he had a pack of pansies there. But he was almost trampled!

The only way he could control them was to block their way and object. "I found it. I get to go up first."

That led to an argument.

Sharon snapped, "How adolescently male!"

"You're not a renter, just a sponger." Petey was sure.

Agnes said firmly, "It's our house!"

But he played a nasty card. "There is probably a phalanx of mice."

"Cray!" It was Sara. "That's not fair. We haven't seen a mouse in ages."

And he replied, "They went to the attic."

So he did get to take the offered flashlight and go up the surprisingly quiet steep stairs. There was another door at the top. That's why it'd been so dark. Cray had to have a can of oil passed up to him before he got the hinges to work and that door to open. They heard it squeak outward. With Cray's threat of mice, that caused gasps.

He walked around the attic. The house had been very solidly built and they could barely hear his footsteps. Finally, he called down, "Come on up. Be careful of your clothes, I can't tell how dirty it is."

They all crept up the stairs. And they looked around, big-eyed and exclaiming. How amazing.

Petey groused, "We've had all this room, all this time. We could have hung our summer things up here."

Cray said, "You still can. I can fix some pipes along the rafters and you can hang things along there. But first, let me clean out the place. I'll open the windows tomorrow and get started. Is it okay if I bring a bedroll and sleep up here? I'll pay a seventh of the rent."

They said, "Great!" and "Okay," but Petey said, "If my mother hears we have a man in the attic, you've got to know what she'll think."

Clay slouched under the ridgepole and said, "Bring her over and let her see how harmless I am."

Most of the women snickered and chuffed, or laughed out loud, but Susanne was oddly indignant and a little testy.

With Susanne still on her proclaimed days off, she decided the next morning that now was a good time to get the whole place cleaned. It took Cray and Susanne two full days to get the attic clean enough to suit her. Then they had to clean the entire downstairs.

Cray objected, "It looks okay to me."

"It hasn't had a real cleaning since last fall. It's spring. It needs to be done while your muscles are here and we can take advantage of them."

With all innocence, he told her, "I have one very agitated muscle that could use some care."

"It just hasn't had any exercise lately, you've done nothing around here, and it'll be all right once we get done."

He sighed with some oddly pent-up anguish. "I can only hope."

They really cleaned. In the bedrooms, they turned beds over onto the next one and thereby had the floor space to really clean.

Susanne worked faster than was smart. She'd never learned to pace herself as a man does who has engaged in tough physical labor. Cray had to give her things to do that wouldn't exhaust her.

When she was out, hanging clean things on the line, Cray took the opportunity to study the picture wall. Among the strangers who belonged to the other housemates, there were pictures of all the Browns and the extended ones.

Cray's two pictures were of a boy of seventeen and one of him in his bush jacket looking out from an outcropping to an uninhabited northwestern Australia. He remembered sending that to Felicia and Salty. He turned it over and saw they'd had it copied.

While Cray fixed the faulty door on the garage, Susanne took his car to the grocery and shopped, and she was the one who made up the casserole for the evening meals in those days.

But she also took down all the drapes and curtains and washed them. They were hung on the wire lines outside, blowing in the good, Texas spring air.

At the end of the day, Cray suggested a good soak in the roomy front-slanted laundry tubs filled with hot water.

Susanne said, "I can't do that. Somebody might come along to read the meter or something."

"I'll watch."

"We-e-e-l-ll—"

He filled the tub for her and let her watch him do that. She ran inside and got some bath oil, shampoo and a special soap.

He took a couple of towels from the clean laundry and waited. She might say, "There's two tubs, why don't you use that one. The Japanese share baths."

But she didn't. He stood around and hinted for a bit, but she was impatient for him to leave her there.

"There are two tubs."

"Now, Cray—"

"I'll have to wait forever. You'll get in that tub and you'll forget all about my poor tired muscles."

She laughed heartlessly.

He chided, "You'd make a terrible mother."

"I'll be perfect."

"You'd work their tiny fingers to the bone and then make them wait while you soak. Heartless."

She gave him an almost salacious look and said, "You're no child."

"I didn't think you'd ever notice."

So he finally, reluctantly left. As he closed the door he coaxed, "Are you sure you're this selfish?"

And she said very sassily and almost flirting, "Yes."

So he walked up and down the sidewalk. Pacing, listening, imagining. And inside that darkened wash-house were the sounds of Susanne slowly moving in the deep water.

He finally got to take his bath. He'd not been entirely sure that his frame would fit into the tub, but it was so deep that he had no trouble. It was hedonistic delight.

While he bathed and soaked out the kinks from the labor, Susanne finished preparing supper. That last cleaning night, she made a fresh vegetable salad with crisp lettuce, croutons and pecans. And there was a fruit compote for dessert.

The workers came home to exclaim over "found" things from corners in the bedrooms. And they were extremely generous in praising all the work the pair had done, because they hadn't had to help.

As if they'd already debated the premise, Petey announced, "Okay, Cray, we'll support you as a house husband."

Susanne's head came up and her eyes got hostile. "Just what do you mean by that?"

Almost too elaborately, Sharon asked Agnes, "Is she being possessive?"

Ellen put in, "She did see him first."

In a gossipy, measured, scandalized way, Sharon commented, "Do you suppose that she's getting over Jack?"

"Sounds like it to me," Agnes agreed. "It's been almost a week."

Petey busily decided, "We can't all have him at once. We need to space our times with him, a little, so we don't kill him off."

Sara suggested, "Let's draw straws!"

"No!"

And the other women laughed at Susanne, while Cray watched her from under lowered lashes.

Could she change her regard from one man to another... that fast? Or was she so insecure that she would need any available man to claim as her own?

Evenings, after working so hard and taking those soaking baths, the pair could barely move. They were so lax and sleepy that considering and speculative looks came their way. Susanne was unaware; however, Cray noted the glances and he was amused.

With their hard days, one thing happened during that time: neither of them had any trouble sleeping, he with his restlessness and she with her grief. It was as he'd planned... almost.

And for the third night, Cray slept in the attic. Being Salty's son, Cray had bought a used flat-bottomed sink. He set it to one side under the roof slant above the first floor bath. He tapped into the pipes below, and he had water. He could rinse off and he had drinking water.

So that weekend, the housemates sorted out-of-season clothing to be hung under cloths on the installed pipes between rafters. Those were on the sink side.

Cray had the rest of the attic. His sleeping bag was arranged under the slant of the other side, and he could walk almost upright in the middle. He bought a secondhand, quite battered but clean three-drawer chest and put that under one window. He too had one of the clothes bars so that he could hang up his things and keep them straight. He'd moved in.

He used the bath in the shed, and he was careful to tap—either way—on the bedroom door before opening it to get to or from the attic.

The housemates said, "You haven't washed the front window."

"I didn't want anyone to know I'm living in the attic."

"Oh." But he could tell that they were puzzled.

There were too many men who walked around the neighborhood. They weren't joggers. Cray had followed some, unobtrusively, expecting them to be from the rabbit-warren apartments over on the hillside, but they didn't live around there. It was a puzzle.

So, on several nights, he went out and walked along Broadway. Sure enough, on the fourth night, the same cop came along. Cray waved him down and said, "Who are the sharks floating around the neighborhood?"

"Well, you gotta know by now that we had trouble with women selling it down the way. We've run them out, but the men think there're still some around. They're sniffing."

"I couldn't find any of them living around here."

"So you've been out following."

"I live with a house full of women an—"

The cop's head came up. "A house full?"

"Yeah. And they're nice women. I'm only visiting for a while, one of the women used to live as a foster child in our house in Ohio. My mother was worried about her and sent me down to be sure everything is okay with her. The women are all good people. I just don't want any strays hassling them. Got any suggestions?"

"Where do they live?"

Cray told him.

"We'll keep an eye on them."

"I'd appreciate it."

And the cop said, "You told them to behave themselves? To close the shades when they aren't dressed? Not to walk at night? Not to go out alone? To look around when they're walking? To keep the house locked?"

"I will."

"Keep your nose clean."

"You sound like my dad, and you can't be any older than I am."

The cop sighed gustily. "In this business, a guy ages fast."

"Maybe you ought to get into another line of work?"

"It's more interesting than adding figures or painting houses."

"My name's Cray Brown." Cray held out his hand.

"I'm Collins. Bart." He shook Cray's hand. "If you ever need us, give my name and tell them to call me."

"I hope I never have to."

"You're alert and have some smarts, I doubt anything would get out of hand. But still, if you need me, whistle—but do it by phone to the station."

Cray laughed, lifted his hand and they parted.

On Sunday, he and Susanne went back to the little church and she paid more attention, looking around and observing. She held her half of the hymnal and sang along.

The preacher announced that next Saturday was painting day. He didn't say any more, so after the service Cray waited until he could ask, "What are you painting next Saturday?"

And the preacher replied, "Oh, well, we find somebody who can't afford the house repairs and painting, and we do it. The paint stores give us a discount. With us all working, we get it done in a day."

"I have some carpentry tools a—"

At Cray's shoulder, Susanne said, "I can paint."

"Fine! You're welcome to come along. We meet here at seven."

"We'll be here." He was inordinately pleased that Susanne had volunteered her own help.

Cray took her out to eat.

She said, "I pay."

"No. I have some backlog, and I've been eating free at your place."

"You bought the roast. You don't have a job as yet. I pay."

"Next time."

So he had his way. They ate at a German restaurant off Alamo Plaza.

After that, they went down along the River Walk and just walked, looking. There was a great deal to see in San Antonio. He felt the need to see it all. That meant he planned to stay awhile. He took her hand in his, and she curled hers around his. It was very nice to walk that way. With her beside him, he felt an unfamiliar sense of peace.

At supper, when all the women were there, Cray told them what the cop had advised. They scoffed at first. Like most women, they never looked around outside. They had found that, as with dogs, a woman should never look a man in the eyes. While a chancy dog felt threatened by eye contact, men took such a look from a woman as a come-on.

"Now wait a minute," Cray objected. "I'm a man, and I'm not hustling you or any threat to you."

"You're living in the attic."

"That's just until I got located. Do you want me to move out?"

And the instant no's were his reassuring reply.

After supper, Susanne asked him, "Is there really danger around here? Should we move?"

"No. The police know about the floaters. They'll be watching. But they can't sit out front in their squad car and not patrol. And you have to protect yourselves. Do as he said. Pay attention."

"Your warning us has made me a little uneasy."

"I'll take care of you."

"Oh, Cray, I'm so glad you're here." And Susanne went into his arms and leaned her softness against him so trustingly that she boggled him.

He understood that she meant nothing inviting. Cray did know that. Maybe she was the kind of woman who turned to any available man so that she could feel protected.

She made him restless. He ought to leave that place. But he already knew that he could not. Not that he would not, he wouldn't leave because he could not.

On Monday, Pepper called Cray. "Your nose still out of joint? I got a couple of motors that need Salty's expertise . . . through you."

"Glad to oblige."

"See you this morning?"

"Yes, sir."

"Good boy."

"Man."

"Right."

So Cray began work. He did one car's motor in short order, then he did the paperwork. Then he showed Pepper how he was fouling up the computer. Then Cray did the computer work. And over several days, he went back and corrected and validated the year's mass of botched records.

Pepper thought he'd struck gold.

But Cray mentioned, "I cost more doing all this mental work."

Pepper was astonished. "Work's work."

"I'll stick with the cars."

"Now, Cray, think how Salty would feel if you did this to him."

"He'd recognize that he needed me and would pay for it."

"Oh, hell. How come wet-nosed kids are so smart these days?"

"They've been taught computers."

Pepper groused as long as he felt obligated to do that, then he settled down and watched Cray get his whole organization organized. It was a pleasure. And Cray made the crew wear clean uniforms daily and do a better job of cleaning up the place and taking care of the tools—and putting them back—precisely.

That included Pepper.

Indignantly, once Pepper protested, "I pay you guys to do the work."

"—and you pay more if a guy has to find a tool that isn't where it ought to be. Time is money."

"Who'd ever believe a hippie throwback tramp like you could be that hard-nosed?"

"You pay me to be."

Pepper looked around. "Yeah." He said with some nostalgia, "The place looks very professional."

"You make a better impression looking professional."

That Saturday, seven o'clock seemed awfully early, but Cray and Susanne did make it to the meeting place at church. The ladies' club had coffee and doughnuts ready. Caffeine and sugar. That would get them started.

The house to be fixed was somewhat tilted into a ravine. Susanne eyed it with dismay. There was no purpose in painting such a house. But there were men who had a big jack, with which they almost immediately leveled the floor, and they put in new, strong posts to keep the house on an even keel.

The men had done it all before, measurements had already been made. They knew what had to be done and how. There was a new window that replaced one ruined by the tilt of the house. And at the other end of the house, the painting had already progressed.

By lunch, there was a great feeling of satisfaction as they sat and viewed what had been accomplished. And the remainder was completed by midafternoon. There were a lot of volunteers.

Cray and Susanne went back to their house for supper, and they took turns bathing in the deep tubs in the washhouse. They watched a film on the videotape machine and were very contented. Well, almost.

Pepper was surprised when a cab company came and negotiated a repair contract. He thought it happenstance. He said to Cray, "How'd they pick us?"

"I talked to them."

And Pepper frowned. He'd talked to them until he was blue in the face. How come Cray could convince them?

Then a car-rental agency did the same. After that, they had to hire some more people to help. They even had a couple of women mechanics, and the men had to watch their language. And it was Cray who interviewed and supervised and decided on those applying.

So in those weeks that passed, Cray could have moved out of the little house. He was making sufficient income to afford a very pleasant place. But he just opened an account at a handy branch bank. He didn't mention to the housemates how well he was doing and how kindly Pepper was treating him.

Cray would come home to the little house, tired and dirty, and he would go back to the bathhouse and soak in one of the tubs. He would eat his supper and he would go to bed early.

The women began to complain. "We never hear anything from you." And they said, "You need to take one day and clean and alternate with cooking us a meal."

He looked at their expectant faces and said, "Okay."

But they knew that he worked longer hours than they, and he contributed his share of the expenses on the dot. He had begun to mow the yard which he kept trimmed, and he cleaned out the bathhouse.

On top of all that, he was their guard.

With the first of March came the Texas celebrating of their independence from Mexico. There were the big parades—the Battle of Flowers was the queen of those. There were enthusiastic parties from casual to ostentatious, and the seven housemates had their own. Cray introduced a couple of the mechanics to the ladies and they were included among the guests. Cray met beginning friends. It was very pleasant, and Cray felt that he belonged.

And on the third Saturday of March, Cray and Susanne again helped in renovating a dying house.

Life was good.

The warmer weather had the spring flowers up and the tree leaves were a mystical green haze on the trees. With the bluebonnets and the verbena blooming, all sorts of sap was rising. And the floaters seemed to wander around more quickly. Or perhaps the women were just aware of them, now that they'd been so seriously warned.

One hot day, with Cray still not home, Petey went to the washhouse and—still dressed—was filling one of the tubs when some man opened the door!

But at that same moment, Sharon came roaring out of the house wielding a broom, yelling at the top of her lungs. The guy fled, vaulting over the back fence, falling behind it. When the two women got there, they could see him limping off across another yard.

The neighborhood dogs set up a terrific din. But no one came to see what was wrong!

That rattled them all. Especially since none of the neighbors had heard anything, with all Sharon's racket! Even with the dogs' hysteria added to the women's hullabaloo, no one had been alarmed. That was unsettling all by itself.

Cray said seriously, "You are not to use the tubs unless I'm on patrol. Got that?" And he called down to the police station, reported an intruder, and he asked that Bart Collins be informed.

The weather became hot. The attic was stifling. Cray bought an air conditioner and put it in the front window of the attic. The women mentioned, "We thought you said you didn't want anyone to know you were living up there."

"This machine can cool the entire house. Cold air falls. Your house will be more comfortable. The neighbors will think you simply want to keep the windows free and the sound away from you."

It was a powerhouse machine. They left the doors open to the attic and those of the other bedroom, and they all slept under light blankets to the hum of the efficient machine. It wasn't even on high power.

And with all the windows and doors locked, Cray slept deeply, restfully, for the first time since he'd moved to the attic.

After he caught up on all the needed sleep and became physically rested, he began to get restless again. He'd waken and prowl back and forth under the ridgepole of the attic, mentally willing Susanne to sleepwalk up the little stair and into his waiting arms and against his willing body.

He dreamed of her. Why her?

He considered all the other five and knew they were intelligent, attractive women. Each was special. Why did only Susanne snare his glance and his thoughts? Why her?

But he'd go home and it was to her. He'd tell things at the table, and it was to catch her attention or to make her laugh. The Friday nights and Saturdays were for laundry, cleaning and visiting. Their days were full of activity.

But Sundays were days of rest. Each Sunday, Cray and Susanne had gone to that little church. Afterward, they'd change their clothes and go exploring around the city, admiring the blending of new with the old treasures. They saw the things that seemed ancient but were actually only a couple of hundred years old.

Everything was relative. The New World was "discovered" five hundred years ago... by the Europeans. It had been known for many centuries to other people. The Europeans only counted time from their point of view.

But the tools and artifacts, and especially the houses and their accoutrements, made the pair of current explorers thoughtful. How crude had been the things available to use. And how difficult it must have been for the first Europeans to live in such inconvenience.

How carefully beauty had been contrived from carved stone and from patterns of colored stone in walkways, and from tin or iron in decorations. It showed their hunger for beauty.

As Cray and Susanne walked together, Cray held Susanne's hand. He would sit them down so that she could rest, and he'd talk to her, touching her hair as if idly. He would put his big hand on her small shoulder and point needlessly, so that he could be close to her.

He loved the scent of her, her own fragrance. He loved the way she looked around, how alert she was. She was like a small, busy bird, but she was a woman and he wanted her.

He liked to sit away from her or to watch her come toward him. She would be unaware so that he could watch her, watch how her body moved and how her breasts jiggled so softly. And he watched the change of her expression when she saw him. Her smile was beautiful, and her face flushed a bit in her delight. It was very heady for a man to see that.

He thought her body was so beautiful that the only thing better would be to see her without those coverings of clothing that she wore.

He knew she was more exquisite than any other woman in the world. He would look at other women and compare them to Susanne, and they were always lacking.

Probably the strangest thing about his feelings for Susanne was that his whole body was especially aware of her. By his skin, he seemed to know where she was, when she was within a certain perimeter.

When they were with other people at the house or in a party of people, he knew exactly where she was.

His back knew if she was behind him. His eyes knew to glance up if she had come into view. It was as if his body was especially sensitive to hers. Yes. While his sex was exquisitely sensitive to her, this other awareness was different. It was strange.

He began to watch her face more than he did her body. He became very protective and tender toward her. He thought he was subtle.

Then the Friday came. They were all at supper, when Agnes said, "We're going up to Austin for the weekend. Do you remember the Houghtons at the last party? They invited us to stay with them. And we're going to a party at a place where the Heavy Weather group is going to play."

Petey questioned Cray, "When you first came here, wasn't it you who introduced us to Bill Small's tapes?"

Cray nodded. "I heard him first on a pirated tape out in California when I was on my way back to Ohio. It was just the tape. No information or address. It wasn't until I was in Cleveland that I knew he was from Austin."

"Can you come along and meet him?" Sara asked.

Cray shook his head slowly. "I have to work tomorrow. Tell him I'm a fan."

"We will." Sharon promised that.

Ellen asked, "How about you, Susanne?"

"That office picnic is tomorrow. I'm on the committee. Tell Bill Small that we all think his music is terrific. Ask him if we can trade this worn tape in for a new one. An even trade, of course."

"Right!" They laughed and said, "We'll buy one and have him autograph it."

Then in a pocket of silence, they all heard as Susanne was quietly asking Sara, "The whole weekend?"

It was Sharon who replied, "Yeah. You two behave."

Everyone laughed, and even Cray smiled. But Susanne and Cray did not exchange even a glance.

Six

___

It was Sharon who said cheerfully, "We'll leave the dishes for you two." The rest of the deserters laughed. When Cray sputtered, Sharon said salaciously, "It'll give you two something to do."

The five were gone within minutes. They took two of the cars, leaving only one in the driveway. Cray could put his car off the street, into the driveway, but he decided against it because, he said, it had become used to being out there.

"You treat that car as if it could think." Susanne teased.

"It can. Don't ever doubt it. I've had it take alternate routes without consulting me." He nodded easily. "There's always a good reason." He then hastened to assure her, "I'm not privileged to know most of them, but on the diverted route, I'll see something beautiful or unusual. On the way down here, the car changed routes because I'd have been held up with a traffic pileup."

"Aw."

"You doubt me?"

"Cars are vehicles."

"—that think. And they talk among themselves at stoplights and parked in malls so they know routes and road conditions. Of course, there are cars that are foolish, just as there are people who are stupid. You have to test-drive a car, so you can figure out if it's smart or dumb."

Susanne grinned.

Cray shook his head. "I can tell, right now, that if you ever buy a car, I'd better be there to help you choose."

"You'd choose an obstinate male one."

Cray raised his eyebrows in a very male way. "So they not only think but they are of a gender?"

"I learned to drive on what had to've been a male car, because it wouldn't do anything my way."

"Uh." He sorted words with some caution. "I see." He hadn't been able to comment without offending her or irritating her, so he'd been smart enough to pass on the comment.

She laughed at him.

He said kindly, "I still have greeting kisses that I was supposed to give you when I got here. My conscience has been bothering me very badly." His voice got ready. "I have wakened in the night, worrying about getting those kisses to you somehow."

She watched him with her cheeks pink and her mouth trying not to smile, but her eyes twinkled and danced with the lights of teasing.

He sighed forbearingly and said, "I could give you a couple now."

And she said, "All right."

His breathing apparatus quit, but he could still manage to move, although it took every available bit of energy to manage that. He put his big hands on her waist and pulled her to him. And he kissed her.

He'd lied. It wasn't any kind of a greeting kiss. It was a lover's kiss. He realized that instantly, and shivered with the knowledge. She would know.

He lifted his mouth and looked down at her face. Her eyes were lazy and the lashes so heavy she couldn't open them all the way. Her cheeks were pinkened and her mouth was red.

Her perfect lips asked, "Whose was that?"

His mind wasn't functioning, and he said, "Huh?"

"Whose kiss was that?"

And he was honest. "Mine."

She smiled a cream-fed-cat smile.

He said in a husky voice, "I only gave you the hello kisses from Salty and Felicia. That was my hello kiss."

"Why did you wait until now?"

"I was afraid if you knew I wanted to kiss you that way, you'd panic."

"Why?"

"Because of the way that I want to kiss you."

"Oh? How is that?"

Well, it was clear to him that he would have to show her, so he kissed her again.

When he lifted his mouth, she was a shambles. He watched avidly as she managed to open her eyes. He had her. He knew he did. She was ready for him. Her lips tried to form the words. She had to struggle with them, but she managed finally to say, "We have to—"

He knew what she wanted. His body was like tempered steel and hardening fast. His muscles were permanently soldered rock.

And she finished. "—do the dishes."

"What?"

"Dishes."

He moved his head back to confirm that she was, indeed, a wrecked and waiting wanton. She was. He said, "You're not serious."

"It has to be done. If we leave the casserole on the plates, we'll never get them clean."

A little annoyed, he asked, "What'd you put in that casserole, glue?"

"No. Why did you think that?"

Well, he certainly wasn't going to touch a tough question like that. He looked at the table and scowled at it. It was a jumbled, abandoned mess. He looked back at his love. She was beginning to release herself from his steel fingers.

And she did manage. That showed— That *proved* that women are stronger than men. How'd she get away from his obstinate grip? She did it effortlessly, even as he watched.

She moved slowly to the table, picked up one dish and floated to the kitchen.

His male logic kicked in, and he knew the only way to handle this problem was to clear the table as soon as possible and get the damned dishes washed. From here on out, they'd use paper plates.

Paper plates? Think of the trees it took to make paper plates! As a confirmed environmentalist, he could not allow the use of paper plates. They'd wash the damned dishes . . . and pollute the ground water.

He carried an almost unbalanced load to the kitchen and found Susanne standing rather bemused and idle in the middle of the room. He didn't immediately register that and told her, "From here on out, we're eating with our fingers."

She wasn't altogether vapid. She questioned, "Soup?"

"We'll drink it from the pan."

By the time they'd washed and dried the dishes, put them away and tidied the kitchen, Susanne was almost back to normal. Cray wasn't. He was just as taut and jumpy as he'd been since catching up on sleep after they got the air conditioner.

As she passed him, he stopped her carefully, turned her toward him and pulled her gently into his arms, against his agitated body. "Where were we?"

She ruffled his hair and said, "I've got to wash my hair."

His mind whirled like the three ribbons on a slot machine. The trio clicked into place and he said smoothly, "I'll help you. We'll do it in the shed."

"We?"

"Um. I've scrubbed hair all my life—" he'd bathed the dogs at home "—and I've become so proficient and practiced, that you'll be in good hands." He licked his lips. "You may call me Pierre." And he smiled, with heavy eyelids, and twirled the moustache part of his beard. He was Salty's and Felicia's own child.

Although she did study him a minute, she went to fetch her shampoo and some towels.

"Get big towels," Cray called from the kitchen door. Then he went to check that the front door was locked. It was not. He did that, met Susanne at the back door and, this time, he locked that, too.

"Why did you do that?"

"No one is around. We are going to be in the shed. Someone could go into the house and surprise us. It's called defensive awareness."

"Not even Salty did that."

"Temple and San Antonio and San Francisco and St. Louis and Seattle and St. Charles are all different places. You do what you have to do. You pay attention."

"How did you think of all those towns that begin with an *S*?"

He drew a steadying breath. "Did you just hear that, or did you understand about paying attention to what I'm telling you women?"

"I've lived here for most of my life."

"You've already heard the cautionings? Same song, thousandth verse?"

She nodded.

"Well, before we get into the gloom of the shed, let's see what I have to cope with here." He stopped her and positioned her and then walked around her, lifting a strand of hair and tsking and umming and sighing. "I just hope I've got you in time."

"Split ends?" She was sassy.

"Hmm." While that was noncommittal, he generously gave her hope. "No mange or flea allergy."

"What? What sort of hair have you been washing?" Then she sobered and asked, "People?"

"Naw. Dogs."

And she laughed.

They were in the shed, and he began to fill one of the two front-slanted elevated washtubs. He told her, "I fixed this short hose for a rinse-off. I wash my hair sitting in the water and the tub's not deep enough for me to dunk down."

"That was a very good idea."

"I have all sorts of ideas."

"You're an inventor?"

He corrected, "Uh... inventive."

That went right over her head. She watched him testing the water on his wrist and said, "I really don't need that much water. There's a pan here on the nail for tiny things or hair washing."

He discarded washing her hair in a little pan. "This is the full treatment. Look on me as you would a medical person. I'm here to help you. You are going to have an experience. You will soak your scaly body in the oiled, heated water, while I give your hair all the attention it needs."

She ran the word over her tongue. "Scaly?"

"When I took your arm, the skin rasped."

"It did not!"

"Oh, yes. Listen." He picked up her arm and ran his other hand over her skin. He made a rasping noise through unmoving lips. "Hear that?"

"You're a con man."

His subtle shock would have made Felicia blink in discreet envy.

The water began to deepen. Cray handled the laundry bottles of bleach, soap and ammonia that sat on the shelf. "No. These won't do for your sk—"

"I should hope not!"

He took her oil bottle and read the directions as he mumbled, "No lemon." And he sighed with disappointed impatience.

"If you were in a lineup of forty men, I would be able to tell that you're a Brown from Temple, Ohio."

"Good-looking?" He smiled with benign assurance.

"Ham. All the way through."

"Disrobe." He said that as if distracted from her by the careful measuring of the oil for the water.

"Huh?"

"Oh, do you soak inside your clothing?" He made it appear that would be a faux pas, and he had dexterously avoided the word "bath."

She considered. She was curious what he would do, how he would react. She wanted to do all those things, soak in the tub and let him wash her hair, but she wasn't sure if she wanted to go beyond that. If she consented to taking off her clothes as he watched, he would probably make love with her. She said, "Cover your eyes."

He immediately put his hand to his face, almost entirely covering his eyes.

"No, you have to use a handkerchief or bandanna."

He lowered his hand in shock. "You don't trust me!"

She closed her eyes, pinched her lips together and enunciated, "Not one sliver."

Mumbling about women and their idiosyncrasies, and what a burden they were to men, Cray sorted through clothes and clean dust rags until he found a reasonable blindfold. He put it on and gasped, "I've gone blind! Alms for the love of God. Alms for the poor."

"Good grief."

"Disrobe."

She eyed him, smiling. Then she began to take off her clothes. She was bent over, taking her panties from her foot when he moved, reaching past her and saying, "I think the water's about to overflow."

She jerked up and looked at the tub as he reached forward, and his hand cupped her breast. "Oh, sorry." And he flapped his hand around until he found the tub and reached in to feel the depth of the water. "It's okay."

"I would have noticed."

"You weren't distracted?"

"Of course not! I would have had to mop it up if it had overflowed."

"You can take off your clothes right here in front of me and not be distracted?"

"You're blindfolded."

"You mean just because I have this on over my eyes." He reached up and lifted it up and looked at her.

"Cray!" She exclaimed as she turned away and wrapped her arms around herself.

He breathed. "My God. You are wonderful!"

She commanded, "Put the blindfold back!"

"Oh, sorry. I was just demonstrating how I couldn't see."

She asked in quick words, "Have you put that back on?"

"Oh, yes." His voice was very earnest.

She turned cautiously and looked at him. His head was down, his eyes covered. "You leave it exactly that way." She was firm about it.

"I promise." He said that with great commitment.

She watched him as she climbed up into the tub. He had straightened and was rigidly still. He was breathing through his mouth. She squinted suspiciously, but she couldn't see his eyes, and the blindfold was in place.

He told her, "Put your back to the divider between the tubs."

His voice sounded strained, and she turned to look at him, but he had his head down and was reaching for a towel. His fingers found it very well, and he began to fold it. She turned her back as she sank into the water and gasped in pleasure.

Her sound set all the hairs on his body rigid and waves of sensation washed over his skin, all of it. He shivered with desire and panted. He tilted his head up cautiously, for he could see down his cheeks along the sides of his nose. And he could see her as she moved her hands and straightened her back so that her breasts tipped up above the water.

She said, "You may begin."

He swallowed noisily and dropped the towel—

"Don't use too much soap."

She meant he could begin *washing her hair.* He reached down and picked up the towel and refolded it.

With his hampered sight, he lifted her head and put the towel under it. Then he put her head back against the towel.

She sighed in pleasure, moving her body again to adjust to the folded towel, and he watched her do that.

"Can't you find the soap? Here. I'll get it for you."

She reached, and he could watch her do that. If he carefully kept his eyes below her shoulders, he could fool her that he couldn't see. He deliberately reached wrong, and she had to shift and turn a little so that she could put the shampoo into his hand. He got to see that, too.

He coughed a couple of times like a flooded engine. Then he settled down enough so that he could begin the shampoo. He put entirely too much of the liquid on his hand, and the excess ran off into the empty tub. He turned on the water and ran the hose around to get rid of the excess and left the water running. The gurgle of the drain screened his odd sounds of panting and twitching.

He began the shampoo. He rubbed in the soap and had a brilliant idea. "Close your eyes so you don't get any soap in them."

She obeyed.

So he busily kneaded her scalp while one hand slipped the blindfold up a way and he could see—everything. He leaned his head back and closed his eyes and asked his guardian angel to leave for a while.

He leaned over behind her head so there was no way that she could catch him watching, and he gave her the slowest, most thorough hair wash any woman in all of history had ever had. He rinsed and soaped and the empty tub was having a hard time getting rid of the excess bubbles.

She was perfectly made. Her body was wonderful. So amazing. It was as if she was the first naked woman he'd ever seen. He was mesmerized. She was exquisite. She was so graceful, so beautifully decorated.

She mentioned, ''If you rub my scalp once more, it will probably begin to bleed.''

He swallowed rather loudly and cleared his throat. ''You really believe it's clean?''

''Past that. Do you have a hair fetish?''

He looked down at the wet blond covering at the apex of her legs and said the hoarse words, ''Selected hair.''

''Well, that isn't too bad. I understand toe men are a nuisance.''

''I've got a lot of soap here, why don't I just go ahead and bathe the rest of you?'' He was astounded by his clever tongue.

Secure, she laughed and said, ''You lecher.''

And he replied, ''Yes.''

She tried to turn her head, but he held it there in place, busily scrubbing. She was unalarmed and commented, ''So you admit to being a lecher?''

''I never was, until just lately.''

''Hmm,'' she said as if thinking, but he could see the little smile on her face and her hands smoothed down over her breasts to her stomach and on to her thighs.

He could do that for her.

He rinsed her hair again. The shampoo bottle was almost empty. He said, ''There's enough soap left for me to wash my own hair. I'll use this other tub.''

"Keep the blindfold on, and I'll do your hair." She shifted. She was doing that so stealthily that he peeked and saw that she was preparing to watch everything he might do.

He got the blindfold back in place in the nick of time. His innovative tongue said, "I'm going to soak, too. I don't mind if you peek at me. But I will wear the blindfold for your selfish sake."

He put the plug into the second tub and started it filling. He then took off his clothes, and she was so avid that he got to watch her watch him. She was curious, and her mouth gave a silent Oh! as his eager sex was released. That silent comment didn't help his control and he had to turn his back and fold his clothes with careful clumsiness as he sought control of his libido.

He got into the tub. She was watching, but she wasn't watching his face. He sank into the water and was smart enough to tilt his head down in anticipation of her glance at his face. He asked slyly, "How do I look?"

She hesitated just that tiny little betraying bit before she asked, "What?"

Wickedly, he accused, "You watched me." He *heard* her smothered guilty gasp.

She asked, "What do you mean?"

"You closed your eyes?"

"Why," she lied. "Of course!"

He laughed.

And *she* laughed!

With that, he took off the blindfold and his humorous eyes looked exactly into hers. He already knew where she was. He shifted and leaned over to kiss her.

She scolded, "You threw away the blindfold!"

"Well, darn. I love your suit."

"Suit?"

"Birthday suit."

"You're not supposed to *talk* about it!"

He looked into the water of her tub and said, "A miracle." His voice was reedy with emotion.

She began to get a little owl-eyed and *her* breathing changed.

"Let me bathe you."

"Oh, no. I couldn't. How can you say I'm a miracle when my hair's all messy and wet."

He looked at her in surprise. "It doesn't matter. On you, a burlap bag would look wonderful."

"But—"

"It's what's inside you, the woman you are inside that makes you beautiful, and you give that beauty to whatever you touch. Touch me."

In a very trembly voice, she asked teasingly, "You want to be beautiful?"

"I want you to think so."

"Oh, Cray... Oh... Cray..."

"I love you, flower child."

"Flower child?"

"Brown-eyed Susanne."

"Cray..."

She was melting. "Kiss me," he coaxed. He leaned over the divider and stretched up, getting to his knees in the tub, and followed after her as she became timid. But she was confined. And with a hand to the back of her head, he kissed her.

It was so tender. He lifted his mouth and looked into her serious eyes. The pupils were so enormous that her eyes looked black. He kissed her again, longer. His hands moved and took her under her arms, lifting her toward him as he kissed her yet again.

He knelt on one side of the barrier and crushed her to him as he lifted her up to meet his embrace. He kissed her with great, head-spinning emotion. It was really a very precarious maneuver and neither even noticed.

He allowed her slippery body to slide down his hairy one, and his eyes were very serious. He said, "We're clean enough."

"I haven't bathed."

"I'll do it."

"Oh, no. I couldn't— You shouldn't— No. Not this time."

The fact that she might let him some other time almost knocked him out of the tub. He said, "Yes."

She was firmer, "No."

"Okay."

"Not *now!*"

"All right. I don't think you understand that I won't bathe you until you say it's okay. Be sure to tell me when that will be."

"Not now."

"I understand. Let me know."

"What?"

"When."

"Oh. All right."

But she looked so uncertain that he wasn't sure she would volunteer the permission. "I'll ask."

She nodded.

He got out of the tub and pulled the plug. He went to her to lift her from the tub, but she shook her head and said, "I'll be along in a minute."

"You want me to leave?"

She nodded.

He was stricken.

She said softly, "Just let me get out by myself and get dressed. I feel shy about my body."

His lips parted in surprise. "With me?"

She pushed her hair back slowly, still watching him very seriously and nodded about twice, sort of.

Solemn, a little puzzled, a bit worried and uncertain, he dried himself off, with glances at her. She did watch him.

He pulled on his discarded clothing and went to her tub. "Don't be long."

Her eyes were so big and serious.

"Don't be afraid of me."

She shook her head a little tremor.

"I'll be outside."

"Yes." She nodded that tremor.

And he went out the door knowing that he wouldn't get to make love to her for a while longer. She was unsure of him. She was shy.

Then he heard the hair dryer.

She was *vain?* She wanted to look good for him? And she thought she needed to dry her hair? My God, what a stupid woman!

But then he realized that water dripping from her hair and down a woman's neck could distract her. It might even be uncomfortable for her. Women were so peculiar that God only knew what they thought or why.

He paced, listening to her movements, and he looked around. The soft darkness was coming. It was late evening. He wondered if there was a really hot film he could use on the videotape machine and heat her up a little. He was about to go out of his mind over this woman.

Why her?

Other than the fact that she was perfect, why Susanne Taylor? And he pondered that.

He suddenly realized there was no sound from the shed. He went carefully over to the door and tapped. "Susanne, are you okay?"

"I'm trying to comb my hair."

"Let me."

She opened the door and looked at him. Her hair looked like a fright wig. On her, it was fantastic. She could start another wave of odd hairdo styles. He had to help her get it under control and save the world from yet another siege of strange-looking women.

"Do you suppose it was too much shampoo?"

"Naw." He was sure. "Here. Let's use some of my beard tamer."

She gasped, "No!" just as he whooshed a couple of quick squirts.

"This'll do the trick," he promised as he rubbed it in. "Doesn't that feel good?"

Under the buffeting fingers and the wild hair, she said, "My scalp is a little tender."

"This'll fix it." He took her brush and began at the bottom of her hair and untangled it. She kept her silence as he squirted one more beard "tamer." Just the word tamer shivered her spine and depressed her. She figured it would all go into a point at the nape of her neck.

She might be able to secretly wash it out in the morning. He was so earnest that she didn't want to hurt his feelings.

Actually, he was very gentle. She allowed him to finish brushing. Her hair would probably all break off and she'd be bald. That would certainly test his attraction for her.

He'd really made it clear that he was attracted.

So was she.

Seven

Susanne's hair was eventually tamed, and she was surprised her head wasn't tender, considering all it had been through at Cray's hands. Her scalp had been rubbed away entirely by his repeated washings. Her hair didn't feel like straw any longer. And more surprising, it didn't feel like his coarse beard.

She said, "Thank you."

He guessed, "For kissing you?"

"For taming my hair."

"If you have any other hair that needs taming...under your arms or along your legs? I'm available."

"You're wicked."

"I'd love to be, but nobody ever taught me how to do that."

She grinned her disbelief, looked at the sky and around at the utilitarian yard. "It's lovely outside." She breathed deeply. Then she elaborated, "—this time of the year." Knowing he watched her, she pointed and had to move her body a little in order to do that. "Did you see the bluebonnets in the corner over there? Petey planted them last November. And they grew!" She was delighted.

"Isn't she from Arizona?"

"Well, yes, but she adapts well to different places. Her daddy was army. What about you, did you adapt well in all the places you've been in these last, was it four years of wandering?"

"Almost four years. No, I was restless and moving on most of the time."

"You certainly saw a lot of the world."

"It's interesting. It's so strange and wonderful, that any traveler knows we have to save it."

"The parents wrote that you're a preserver."

"Most people are."

"You take it very seriously."

"It needs to be taken that way. We have no other planet."

They walked slowly around the backyard, with Cray slowly ducking under the permanent wire clothesline. She was shy. He'd known that all along. He took her hand and held it in his.

She allowed that.

"We have the weekend."

"Yes."

"Come inside and let me show you how nice this can be."

She didn't move her head as she looked all over the yard in that direction. "Is the man supposed to say it that way?"

"I don't know."

"Have you made love to a great many women?"

"Not that I recall."

"But you have?"

"I don't think so."

"You would have to remember something like that."

"I must not have at all. I sure don't remember any woman as special and tempting as you."

"I don't mean to tempt you."

"I know you don't."

"But I do remember wishing you'd look at me the way you looked at Clara Borden."

He frowned. "Clara? What Clara? Neal's sister?"

She nodded. "You were sixteen and you...mooned over Clara. You slicked your hair down and put your stocking cap on to hold it just that way."

"I never did that."

"Oh, yes. I was terribly jealous."

He swung her hand a little and said, "I've got a stocking cap in the trunk of the car. I'll go get it and slick my hair down and put on the cap and drive you crazy with lust. And I'll do my best to satisfy that lust."

"I have no interest in you at all."

"Oh, yes, you do. You watched me undress and get into the tub. You stared."

"I did nothing of the sort." She shook her head, lifted her chin and looked down her nose at him.

"I saw you."

"You were blindfolded."

"I could see from under it, along my nose."

"You *couldn't!* Not really?"

"Yes."

"Why, Cray! I'm shocked!"

"You should have seen what you did to me.... And you did see."

She put her hand over her face and blushed scarlet, but she laughed!

"I need to give you some more family greeting kisses. Tom; new brother-in-law, Luke—"

"You've already pulled that twice. I'm not that slow."

"I want to kiss you."

She blushed a little and smiled secretly. "I think I might be able to handle—one."

"I can't kiss you properly out here. All the neighbors are sitting on their roofs with field glasses and watching."

She looked around. "No, they aren't on their roofs."

"They are on the other side of the peaks." He told her gravely.

She grinned and shook her head. "What do you mean you can't kiss me 'properly' out here? I should think, with the witnesses you claim are watching, that 'proper' would be the only way you could kiss me."

"It's semantics, the understanding and verification to the meanings of words."

"Uh, you mean that your definition of 'proper' might not be mine?"

"I'm older and more worldly. The meaning has ramifications."

She laughed in pleasure with his words.

And he thought what a jewel she was. Her laugh tickled along inside his body and played with the pitch of his desire.

"You have to think of another reason for me to go inside the house." Choosing her words carefully and searching for the exact ones, she managed to tell him: "If I go in with you now... you will assume that I'm... a willing... participant in your... interpretation of 'proper' kissing."

He put back his head in order to laugh his delight at her response. But it wasn't a shouting laugh, it was throaty and extremely humorous and intimate. It had been just for her ears.

His reaction pleased her beyond reason. She twitched and peeked at him and rubbed her nose to hide her smile.

So he was grinning as his eyes seemed to dance with lights of humor. He then said, "I'm hungry."

She considered the newly presented reason. She moved for his observance, turning her head and twitching her body and forcing him to watch her. She was enjoying the fact that he did watch.

He had a very hard time not grabbing her and hugging her in a breathtaking crush, she charmed him so much.

Then she said, "Well, I sup-pose—" and she drew out the word quite decidedly "—we'll just have to take you inside... and... feed you." She looked at him, knowing he watched avidly.

He shook his head helplessly. But he knew there was no question that he loved this child-woman more than any human in his life, and more than his own. She was the answer to his restlessness, she was the pivotal part of his existence. Without her, his life would go back to being dust.

They moved gently to the back door. There were three steps up to the platform that was the back porch. Cray reached to unlock the door for her and to hold it open.

She entered rather formally as if, in crossing the threshold, she crossed a line that had serious meaning.

He followed, closed and locked the door before he turned to look after her. His face was serious.

She moved into the dining room before she stopped to wait for him. He reached for her, but she put a hand on his chest. She said, "I'm not a virgin."

He replied, "Neither am I."

She made no comment, but just looked at him.

He asked, "Was it Jack?"

"No. It was . . . my stepfather."

"Ah-h." Her reply explained many things. Her being in the Brown house, and the care and concern of Salty and Felicia. The reason Salty had been the one who'd returned her to her mother was because they had needed to know that Susanne would be safe.

Cray gave up any sexual blending at that time. He needed to be sure she was not only willing, but that she would be all right. He took her hand and led her into the living room. He sat on one end of the lumpy sofa and patted his thighs. "Come sit down."

That gave her the choice of the intimacy of lap sitting or she could choose to sit beside him.

She did hesitate, then she went to him and carefully sat on his lap.

He was immeasurably touched that she could trust him so much. It made him a mush of tenderness toward her, and his enclosing arms and hands were excessively gentle. He kissed her cheek.

"Whose greeting is that?"

He had to realign his thinking. He'd promised to give her family kisses. "Well, you have to remember that Salty only knuckles heads and wobbles shoulders?"

"—and Felicia kisses foreheads or the air by cheeks. That's how come I suspected something fishy in those two greeting kisses you gave me the first day, which were supposed to have been from them."

"You're a clever, wily woman. Are you sure you don't work with the police department?"

"No. Just city records and statistics."

"Are you going to kiss me?"

And she put her arms around his head and kissed him as if it were the first shared kiss between a man and a woman. It was such an amazing happening. It was exploring and sharing and thrilling. How could one simple kiss hold such meaning?

He held her to him and groaned and his lap got bumpy. He said, "I think we, maybe, should go for a walk."

She swallowed rather noisily and suggested, "Let's go up in the attic and see if the air-conditioning is working properly."

He quit groaning and froze, his mind whirling. She was inviting...? He pulled his head back and looked down at her in his arms and asked, "Are you sure?"

She was a little nervous. Her nod bobbled somewhat, but her serious eyes were steady.

He helped her rise, then she had to help him. He walked as if full of kinks. He was so uncertain, that he didn't know how to act. If he did anything wrong, it could ruin this fragile girl woman. It could harm her emerging acceptance forever.

He asked gently, "Have you had counseling?"

"Forever. The last one said, 'You can dwell on that incident the rest of your life, or you can go on. It's like being thrown by a horse. Will you never ride another horse? Or will you choose one that will allow you to ride with the wind.' That was several years ago." She smiled a little. "I believe I'd like to... ride you."

She paralyzed him. What if...she couldn't stand it? What if it should devastate her? What if he frightened her? What if—

Watching him earnestly, she interrupted him. "When you undressed out in the shed," she said seriously, "and I saw you, I thought you were beautiful. I knew, then, that it would be all right, if it was with you."

His eyes prickled and became shiny with tears. His smile was so tender.

She said, "Oh, Cray. You are just the sweetest man." She flung herself into his arms and held him. "You have been so nice to me. I couldn't believe how tolerant you were and how wonderfully you helped me to get past being dumped by Jack. You did everything right. How did you know how to do that?"

"If it worked, then it was right. If it hadn't, we'd have tried something else."

"That's the way Salty and Felicia did. But mostly, they loved me. And Salty showed me how men can be. He is a very special man. Do you know that he writes

me a note every week? Just a line or two telling me to
work hard, keep my nose clean and to pay attention.
Felicia's letters are so wonderful, full of gossip and
news, and I love them, but Salty is the one who got me
to see men as they can be. You are such a man."

"I'm not at all like Salty."

"You're still rebelling and competing. Felicia says
when you mature, you'll be just fine."

"What?" he huffed.

And she laughed. She stood there and laughed such
a lovely, amused sound, then she wrapped her arms
around his shoulders and pressed against him. "I'm
so warm, I think the air conditioner is on the fluke. We
probably ought to go up and see."

"My knees are wobbly. I'm not sure I can make it."

She sighed, "I've heard that women can carry men
in a fireman's hold. Shall I try?"

"No. Just give me your hand."

"My heart's in it. Take my hand and you take my
heart with it."

"It's safe with me."

"I know. That's why I've chosen you."

"You chose Jack first."

"I was impatient. I thought you were never going to
come back."

"I'm here."

She hesitated just a shade, then she moved her body
in a nice shift and commented, "It's so *warm* in here."
She blew up on her face and held him one-handed, as
she used the released hand to fan her face as she gave
him a smug and wicked look. Then she said, "When
you got to northwestern Australia and began to emote
about the vast spaces of cleanness, your parents wor-

ried that you'd decide to stay there. They said you would come back for Bob's marriage to Jo."

"Now, how could they know he was going to marry her?"

"From the time he asked if he could come home after his divorce out in Boston. They picked Jo to distract him." She let her arms slide down his chest as she pulled her head back to look up at him. "Have you lost interest?"

"You have me so nervous about hurting you, that I probably couldn't have made love to you anyway."

"Aww. I didn't mean to affect you that way. I thought to reassure you. You needed to know that I wouldn't cop out at the last minute."

"I hadn't remembered why you were at our house."

"I should have thought of that. You really don't remember me."

"I don't think it's that, so much as it is that some of the kids had had even worse times than you did. Your experience was bad enough. Do you know what you're doing to me? If you don't know, you ought not to go upstairs with me."

"I do know. I want to go upstairs to your sleeping bag and make love to you."

"You scare me spitless."

"A grown man like you?"

"Yeah."

"Well, if this is how you work it so that I'll seduce you, let's get started."

"Susanne—"

"God, how I hate it that I'll have to take you by force!"

He shook his head and laughed.

"I absolve you of all responsibility. I even bought a supply of condoms. I'm not sure I can put one on you. When I saw you naked, it seemed to boggle around quite a bit, but I will try. Doing that is probably a lot like being able to rope a calf?"

"If you'll hold it steady, I can put on a condom."

"Have you used very many?" she asked with polite interest.

"No."

"Well, I've had only that one experience, and he didn't use one, so we'll have to muddle through together." Then very kindly, she asked, "Are you willing to be an instructor?"

He was cautious. "I'm not sure."

"Well, let's go see if you can be convinced."

"Are you sure?"

"Good grief! This is my idea. I need to know whether or not I can make love with you."

"Do you mean this is a test?" He huffed a little.

"Actually, yes."

"And you're going to *grade* me?"

"I suppose you could say that. But you can grade me and be critical, too. And we might work on this aspect of togetherness . . . together."

Only then did he realize exactly how brave she was being. His hands became gentle and he lost his cautious manner. "We probably should go up and start testing. You may have to work a little to get me willing."

"I've read a book." She soothed him.

He stopped walking. "I think I could be terrified."

"Relax. I know what I'm doing."

"I feel as if I'm walking to the guillotine."

"Oh, for Pete's sake! You can sure tell who are your parents. How dramatic! It won't be *that* bad."

"Are you sure you aren't after me because you've exhausted all the men in San Antonio?"

"You're my second. I've told you that, but you're my first that I've wanted and want to try out. It looks like it could be a lot of fun and very interesting, from the book."

"Where is this book?"

"Under my mattress."

He watched her. "Maybe I ought to read it first so that I can know what you're going to do and I can be . . . braced."

"I would never believe you could be this timid."

Still standing in the dining room, he said, "Hah!" And he said, "'Timid' to you, is 'careful' to me." And he said, "You're probably voracious, and I will be depleted and used up by morning."

She took several steps toward the hall. "I'll pace us very carefully."

Not moving, he accused, "You say that because you're still 'selling' and you don't want me scared."

She became serious, knowing about being scared. "Do you mean that? Do I frighten you?"

"I'm just making you sweat. You deserve it for plotting my downfall without even asking me."

"Well, you're twenty-six. You're on the downhill side of sex, having peaked at nineteen. I will preserve and protect you, pacing you so that you don't fizzle out."

"Your word choices are just dandy."

"Dry up?" She substituted helpfully.

"How can you be such a skilled dramatizer?"

"Now, you *know* I had two years with Salty and Felicia. I was in an absorbing stage at age ten and eleven."

In a different voice that was very gentle, he asked quite seriously, "Are you sure about doing this?"

And she replied airily, "Do you realize my housemates had begun to quarrel about who was going to get you? I really had to muscle them down and drive them back. You're a gem. They all recognize that."

"Are they really in Austin this weekend?"

She nodded. "And they're going to see Bill Small's Heavy Weather group play. It was you who made us aware of that group. So when the opportunity came to go up and see them play, the others agreed to go."

After a slight pause, Cray repeated, "They... agreed... to go."

"Uh, well, yes. I saw where the group was to play, and it seemed a great opportunity to get the five out of the house so that I could seduce you."

"You deliberately *planned* it for *that* long?"

"Yeah." She gave him an interested, logical look.

Pensively, he absorbed the fact. Then he speculated, "I wonder how many men in this world think they've set up a seduction and never know they were the victims."

"Aw, do you feel put upon?"

He didn't reply immediately. He looked at her and his eyes became lazy. He said, "Not yet."

She took a step toward him and reached for his arm. "Come along. I'll show you how to be put upon."

He allowed her to tug him into the hall. "You admit you never intended to examine the air conditioner?"

"Oh, sure, we could have stood in front of it long enough for me to cool down a little."

"You're being very rash."

"I'm a few other things, too. Like willing." She tugged him another step.

"What are you going to do with me, once we're up there."

"Chapter one."

He stopped walking again. "The whole chapter."

"Yep."

"I think I ought to see the book."

She tugged again. "I hate people who read ahead. I like to go page by page . . . and savor the experience."

"I bet you're all talk."

She gave another little tug. "I'm the one coaxing you along."

"How do I know you're not just a tease?"

"I guess you'll just have to find out."

He took another step. She bragged on him. He allowed her to maneuver him into the bedroom and shift the doors so that he could go up the attic stairs, following her. She turned back and waited as he emerged into the attic.

He surveyed his own things—the racks of covered clothing, the freestanding sink and the efficient air conditioner. He pronounced, "It's a den of inequity."

She also examined the premises. "A good friend of mine lives up here."

"He's probably a deadbeat."

She defended him to himself. "He's working at a job."

Cray had never told her that he was gainfully, well employed, at Pepper's auto repair. He said of himself, "So he isn't working?"

"Not regularly."

Cray carried it on. "His problem is probably his beard."

"No, that makes him distinguished looking."

Cray continued, "I've seen the guy. He has small ears and thin lips. He's probably stingy and cold."

"I intend to test that premise."

"When?"

"Now." She was businesslike. "Take off your clothes." She gestured openly, then stood and watched him.

He was appalled. "No preliminaries? Just...strip? Is that what your book says to do?"

"Well, I've already seen you naked. I didn't think you'd turn shy on me."

He sighed heavily and shrugged. "Show me how you want it done. To music? To simple hand clapping?"

She laughed without opening her lips. Her eyes were sparkling and she was pink-cheeked and attentive. She was utterly charming. "Take off your shirt first."

"All the women I've seen get a man out of his clothes, do it themselves. They flirt and unbutton buttons and slide their hands inside his shirt and—"

"I hadn't realized that. I guess I could do that. Here. Let me."

"Wait a minute. You have to kiss me a couple of times and get me interested."

"You're not?"

He looked off down the attic. "You have to catch my attention."

She put her hands onto her forehead as she leaned her head into them, and she paced away from Cray as she said, "How to get his attention? Hmmmm. Now, what did the book say about that?" She looked up at him and bit the side of her lower lip as she scratched under her breast making it tremble.

"Hmmmmm," she said, turning away from him and putting her hands on the back of her hips, to stand with her feet apart, as she leaned her head back and looked up at the rafters meeting at the ridgepole.

Then she turned back toward him and ran her hands down her hips as she licked her lips. "I suppose I could kiss you?"

"You could try it." He sounded as if he didn't think that would work.

But she didn't come to him. She put her lower lip up over her upper lip and surveyed him. Then she thoughtfully put her index finger into her mouth to bite it in contemplation, as she tilted her head down, a little, and looked at him with big, considering eyes.

He asked in a husky voice, "Do you think I'm made of iron?"

"Actually," she said slowly. "From what I've seen of you, I do."

"You're tearing me apart. You're a tease."

She looked surprised. "I'm just trying to think how I'm going to take off your clothes."

"And you were kind enough to mention that very idea before you started driving me wild—"

"Are you wild? Why?"

"—posing and tempting me."

"Am *I* doing that?"

"You know you are, don't you?"

"Well, I have been practicing in the bathroom mirror for several weeks."

"Several *weeks?* Why didn't you mention it to me?"

"Oh. Were you supposed to know? I thought I'd take you by surprise."

"You've acted like I wasn't anything any different than all the other housemates."

"I've kissed you every Sunday, while we were going around the city."

"Nice little sweet kisses."

"You didn't like them?"

"They weren't enough."

"Tell me. Show me—"

"Come here."

"—as soon as I get your shirt off."

"Here, I'll—" He started unbuttoning it.

"No, no, no, no! I'm going to do that."

"Well, get to it, then."

"You're hurrying things along too fast."

"I believe you're testing my patience. You're seeing just how far you can push me. You think you're in complete control, when you have no idea how chancy I am right now. You need to realize that I'm a human man, and I have limits."

She lifted her chin and gave him a cool look. "And you have superb control. You will wait until I'm ready. I want to do this my way."

"Good luck."

"I'm going to unbutton your shirt."

"You don't announce it, you just *do* it."

"How many women have undone your buttons?"

"You're talking shirts, right?"

"What other buttons are there?" She looked down his front. "Your jeans?"

"Haven't you ever heard about a woman pushing a man's 'buttons' by controlling him? You're pushing mine. I'm just warning you that I have limits."

She considered. She walked around beyond his hands' reach and contemplated the fact that he had limits. And she was deliberately pushing those limits. She turned her head and glanced over her shoulder. She walked past him and gave him cool looks from under half-lowered eyelids.

She was wickedly enflaming.

Eight

—

Then Cray remembered the troubled child of ten years ago who had been Susanne. And he compared that fragile victim to this carefully built, strong woman. He could only be awed by Susanne's recovery.

He had to be careful of her. He had to forget his hunger and help her to open the barrier of her own protected bastions.

He figured that she hadn't meant to torment him so much as she was seeing if he would force her. That was what she expected. She was unsure of her own reaction. That was why she stayed out of immediate reach. With all her boldness, she was still uncertain.

He knelt down, opened out his arms and said in a soft, husky voice, "Love me."

She was stopped in her tracks, her face went blank and her lips parted in surprise. She went to him and knelt down in front of him. She put her arms around him and lifted her mouth in surrender.

He didn't enclose her, but kept his arms to his sides. He gently kissed her in sips, softly and sweetly. He kissed her longer, then longer, more thoroughly. He turned his gentle mouth, coaxing her lips to part. His tongue touched and slid along, asking her to open to him.

His tongue felt her lips tremble in nerves. He went back to squishy kissing. Her mouth opened timidly and about unmanned him. Maybe... *over* manned. And their kiss, then, shook the universe.

They sighed and gasped. They shivered and trembled. They got each other out of their clothes without any calculation, rhyme or reasoning. They lay naked on his bedroll in straining writhings, their heat putting the air conditioner on overload.

And she was urging for the coupling, her eyes closed, her breaths panting, her legs and hands grasping, when Cray stopped because something wasn't right. He finally remembered the condom.

As she made little protesting mews, he had to untangle and grope and reorient and figure out where they were and what condoms looked like.

They calmed a little and solved that. Then they sat panting, looking at each other in almost wildness. And Cray smiled.

With their breaths still panting and restless, she smiled a little. He laughed a naughty, marvelously intimate chuckle. And she grinned a bit bigger. Then he waggled her head with one hand, messing her hair even more. And she joined in his laughter, threw her arms around him and kissed him a wonderful con-

suming kiss that was as free, as unfettered as her released spirit.

She had expected that he would then take her. She
had cooled with his search for the condom. Now she
braced herself, sobering, a bit wide-eyed, and waited
for him to roll over on top of her and complete the act.

She stiffened involuntarily and tried to relax. She
was a little disappointed. She was sorry they hadn't
foolishly gone ahead without the condom. She would
have probably enjoyed it, then. She waited to endure
his taking.

He didn't. He, too, was somewhat cooled, and he
could think again. He saw that she was wary. There
was no way that he'd take his release from her at that
point. He could ruin all her carefully structured brav-
ery, and dead memories might begin to live again. He
wanted her so hot that she would think of nothing but
him, so he delayed.

He kissed her in those honeyed sippings. He ran his
palm over her ivory cheek. He slid his fingers into her
hair and kissed her eyelids. He drew a line down her
shoulder, across one breast, over her pale nipple, down
into the valley between those mounds, up and across
the other breast and nipple and up over her other
shoulder. She watched him do that.

He nuzzled that beard along her throat and under
her ear. He kissed her nicely, his mouth a soft surprise in that perfectly textured beard. Then he leaned
and gently rubbed his beard on those rounds. There's
something about male hair—chest or leg or whatever—that excites women's bodies.

He found that the underside of her knee was susceptible to his beard, the inside of her elbow loved it.

Her armpit, her stomach, the insides of her thighs were equally vulnerable.

His hands moved on her as he worked her, smoothing, feeling, touching. He lifted his mouth from hers to watch his hand, and her own gaze followed his exploration.

He made murmuring sounds as he rubbed her in intimate places and watched as she closed her eyes. Her lips became a small soft *O*, as she slowly turned her head or lifted her chin or moaned. And her sighs and gasps and pantings filled him with pleasure.

He took his glistening finger from her and drew the tip of it up the middle of her body, down into her navel and up her breasts to circle both now scarlet nipples before he ran it up her throat and to her mouth. He touched the finger to her lips, but then he put that finger into his own mouth while he watched her.

She was sober as she witnessed that.

Then he lay her back and gently entered her, shivering with his control. She was a liquid inferno and she scorched him in her dancing fires. He warned her, "Hold still!"

But she was lost to desire, to her passion. She clutched him with her arms and wrapped her long legs around him, groaning with need.

And they were whirled helplessly up that narrowing spiral into the sensual oblivion of rapture. They clutched each other as their hair seemed to fly with the wind in the vortex and their ears were filled with roar of the sounds of the rush.

They came to, panting, lax as boneless soft plastic. Surfeited. Gasping. Ruined.

When she could make sense, she said quite soberly, "No wonder."

That confused him, but he hadn't the energy for questions.

He finally managed to pull a summer blanket up over them, and they slept in total oblivion.

He wakened in the night with a dead arm and an excited sex. He'd tried to turn over and found himself trapped. A dead weight on his dead arm. Then he remembered. She was there. She was with him, still. And his body had already known that and rejoiced.

Under the sound of the humming air conditioner, Cray smothered his chuckle of amazement. He had been soundly asleep but his eager body was ready. That precious woman was there beside him. Available?

He eased his arm from under her, went naked down the stairs to the bath and disposed of the used condom in the kitchen trash. He went around the lower floor, looking out, checking. Everything was quiet. He went back up the stairs like a phantom.

In the darkness, by then, he knew to put up a hand to prevent his head from bumping on the low rafters. With some anticipation, he eased under the blanket and found her warm, lax body. He sighed in sensual delight, "Ahh."

She yawned and stretched, moving her fascinating body within his hands, before she relaxed and asked lazily, "Who are you?"

"A *very* good friend."

She chuckled nicely. Then she gasped and said, "That is unusually friendly." And after a rustling, busy minute, she said, "Now, that's pretty forward!"

"You want to see 'forward'?"

"Good grief. You have a real problem."

His husky voice promised, "It can be solved."

And she laughed. But she helped. "You are just so interesting!"

It was dark, and she could explore him more easily. She thought he couldn't see her. But he had cat's eyes.

She threw back the light blanket, and he watched the movement of her body, the grace of her arms, the wiggle of her breasts as she did that. She moved around, seeking, testing, tasting, curious. He missed witnessing some of her movements because her ministrations sometimes closed his eyes as he groaned.

Her body was a ghostly presence, her faintly dotted breasts wiggled and moved, her graceful arms and legs shifted. Her bottom was rounded and sweet, the silk of her pubic hair was so blond that it seemed roughened skin which shielded her so inadequately.

He allowed her the freedom of him, and he was almost paralyzed by her exploration. It was the tasting that riveted him and made hoarse sounds come involuntarily from his throat. His fingers dug into the sleeping bag and his toes curled.

He told her, "You're killing me."

"I know. I can tell. But I'll heal you pretty soon."

"Uh...how...will you...do that?"

"I'll show you in a minute."

"How did you learn to do that?"

She pulled her mouth off his nipple with a smack, and replied, "From you. You did this same thing to me."

"Not the book?"

"It wasn't as interestingly presented in the book as having you demonstrate the skill to me."

And another time, with his toes curled so tightly that he'd never again be able to wear shoes, he asked gutturally, "How did you...know...to do...that?"

She pulled her mouth from him slowly and licked her lips. "It just seemed logical."

"I like a logical wo—" and he gasped and swallowed noisily and shivered.

When he was about to swing from the rafters, she took pity on him and fitted her amazing body on top of him and squirmed around until his eager sex was completely, hotly sheathed. But as he anticipated release, she didn't move.

He mentioned, "I'm going crazy."

"This is fascinating. I had no idea the power of sex. You really are just about desperate. You are helping me to understand many things."

He blinked and opened his mouth, but she moved...a little.

She said, "I'm enjoying playing with you. If you get terribly uncomfortable, you can turn me over and finish it. Okay? I don't want to torment you."

"I don't mind this kind of torment. But be careful, the rocket could go off and I could blow you right through the roof."

She chuckled low in her throat, and just the sound of it sent flicks of fever through him and his molten blood became thicker and heavier. His sex was swollen, filling her tightly, and he fought for control so that she could play with him a while longer.

She leaned over and dropped a nipple into his mouth, and he sucked hard, feeling the double contact. He let the nipple go with a pop and took the other, making her moan with sensation.

She sat up making him lose the nipple, and she moved her hands over his body, feeling, she curled and suckled his own nipples as she moved her hips in a slow, hot swirl. But she laughed again as he groaned.

He reached for her shoulders and pulled her to him to lay her flat on him as he bent his head to kiss her, their tongues touching, petting, probing.

Without separating, he carefully rolled them over and began to move, with exquisite stealth, his body rigid with want. She clutched him, straining to taste ecstasy again.

He stopped. His breath labored. He levered up onto his elbows and said, "You were a witch. You are so thrilling, I forget the condom. We can't go on this way. I've got to be more careful. I can't imagine being so careless. I—"

"You're babbling."

He carefully pulled away from her gripping body, her scrabbling, protesting hands and her locked ankles. "Let go," he groaned the words.

"You're right." She reluctantly relaxed and allowed him to separate from her.

He sat, collecting his scattered, swirling thoughts so that he could coordinate his movements. He carefully moved to his hands and knees, mindful of the rafters, but then he leaned over and kissed her. "Don't move."

"Cover me up, I'll freeze."

"If you cool off, we get to start from scratch."

"I never scratched you." She was indignant.

"Uh . . . Start from the beginning?"

She turned away as if indifferent. "I don't think I have the energy."

"I'll help."

He covered her enough. Then he crawled away to find the condom. When he returned, she pretended to be asleep, but she sighed theatrically, stretched too temptingly and turned to display herself to him. This woman did all that not even eight hours after she'd made him wear a blindfold. He didn't mention that.

So he put his head down and nuzzled around, sampling what he could find. She twitched, as if annoyed, and turned away slowly and made him work. He loved it.

Her skin was soft and smooth to his hand, so different from the feel of his own. The inside of her thigh was so tender and sensitive. His gentle hand was harsh on that sweet flesh.

He coaxed her.

She said in a pout, "My tongue's sore from kissing."

So he sought to capture it and sucked it and kneaded it with his own.

"My chest's cold from the air conditioner."

He paused. How could that be with his hairy chest smothering her sweet, soft breasts? Who cared? He shifted from her chest and his hand worked and kneaded the rounds. And he gave further attention to that area of need. Then he rubbed his face slowly in the little canyon between the mounds, licking and mouthing, and his attentions went on down to her navel, which might have been chilled, but was not. And he extended his considerations farther.

She helped. She moved, when he wasn't quite on the mark, and she held the back of his head. She sighed and arched her back, and she was diligent in her assistance.

And when it was needed, she parted her knees and welcomed him.

By then, he was so hard that he was especially gentle to her tender flesh. He eased himself so carefully, and he was being pleased with his care of her, when she curled to meet him. Her hand hit his lower back and grabbed him in a tightening pressure that was astonishing.

He slammed into her, and the race was on! Fevered, but short. She was voracious and a cauldron of demand, which he met with some astonishment and a great deal of delight. He rode her out. Rode until she began to relax with sighs of fulfillment. And he could not have possibly sustained the intense level of excitement all that time, but he'd never been so drained.

He collapsed and lay inert. Finished.

After a short time, she said, "You've gained some weight."

He couldn't believe she could have changed from the screeching witch who'd tried to claw him closer...to this rejection. He levered himself to one elbow. The other elbow wasn't doing anything practical, it was the dead arm that had begun the whole episode. He asked, "Are you okay?"

And airily, she said, "For now."

He laughed helplessly and lay back down on her.

She said saucily, "Not now." And she pushed at him in a token rejection with no energy at all.

He withdrew from her and lay depleted. No threat. That was the last he knew until morning.

He wakened sticky, and feeling lazy. He yawned and stretched, and found she was still with him. She was lying on her stomach, her chin popped on one hand, feisty and smug.

She said, "I suppose I've depleted you entirely? What will we ever do with all the rest of this weekend? They won't be home until tomorrow evening! And here you are—" she looked at her watch "—at ten o'clock, with two full days to go, and you're barely wiggling."

He put a hand to his forehead and said in a tiny, weak voice, "Food."

"I swear, I've never seen such a dramatic man. I suppose the only thing I can do is try to keep you alive. What do you want? Eggs, cereal, pancakes?"

"That'll be enough to start."

"All of that?"

"Yes. I've been warned. I need to keep my strength up."

"Don't you have to work today?"

"Naw."

"You *said*—"

And he countered: "What about the picnic?"

"I called in sick—with love, of course—but I didn't say that. I just said I had to spend the weekend in bed." She gave him a precious look.

He pretended to faint.

She laughed with appreciation, kissed him and then had to struggle to get away. "I thought you were helpless."

"I am! I am!"

She poofed that in disbelief, then declared, "I get the shower first."

"Let's bathe in the tubs."

"Not this morning."

"I could give you a sponge bath here," he offered with such kind innocence.

"Sure. If I agreed to that, I'd never get downstairs, and I'd starve."

He offered, "I could bring you a tray."

"I don't eat trays. I eat food."

He said a forlorn, "Oh."

"I'll pound on the door when I'm finished in the shower."

"Leave a little hot water. I'm sore and used up."

She stopped and turned her head to look at him. "Are you okay?"

"Of course. I was trying to get you back within arm's reach."

"Lecher."

"How could you know that so fast?"

"I just spent a night with you. You are a shockingly sexy man. I can't believe I've escaped your clutches this long."

"You've had all those chaperons cluttering up the place."

"That's why we're all here. There's protection in numbers."

"You didn't mention any numbers last night."

"Not numbers as numbers, but numbers of women around. That's the deterrent to lecherous men."

He stretched luxuriously and said with satisfaction, "I can't tell you how glad I am that they weren't anywhere around last night. Or this morning."

She reached over, ruffled his hair and gave him a sweet kiss.

He allowed her to escape, watching her pick up her clothing and go naked down the stairs.

He sighed in great contentment. He heard the sounds in the bath downstairs. The shower ran for quite a while. Then it was shut off and he waited for her knock on the door. He almost went back to sleep. When the knock came, he hauled his sated body out from under the summer quilt, and noted that it wasn't as sated as he thought it should be. He chided, "Greedy." And it bobbed in agreement.

He straightened the bedroll and blanket, then folded them to take them down to air outside on the line.

He gathered the clothing he needed and went down to shower. It felt great. He dried his body and put on clean clothing, feeling remarkably fit and virile. Especially virile.

In the kitchen, Susanne was busy and humming. Seeing her there and seeing her happy gave him a greater feeling of contentment. She greeted him with a smug little smile and allowed him to give her a kiss, but not the concentrated double whammy that he wanted to share.

"Sit down," she said bossily. "I've had to wait and wait for you."

And she fed him enough for three and a half starving men.

"You trying to keep my strength up?"

She chewed busily, licked her fascinating lips and replied snippily, "Yes."

Any woman who is that sassy needs some man's attention. He knew that, and he felt pleasure radiate through his body and decided he was exactly the right man to handle this snippy, sassy woman. This woman who had plotted his downfall. They'd just have to sort out who was in control here.

After breakfast, Cray couldn't move for almost forty-five minutes, he was so stuffed. Susanne talked to him and entertained him and flirted with him, catching his attention.

She showed him the packet of letters she'd had from Salty, and the stack of family letters from Felicia. But Salty's letters were just to Susanne, while Felicia's were the Xeroxed copies to everyone. It was she who had kept all the clan in touch. How many personal letters had Salty written to his children?

And Cray remembered the ones he'd received. Always succinct and to the point. Mind your manners. Do your share. Keep your honor clean. Look carefully at your companions. The admonitions had irritated the liver out of Cray, but he had paid attention.

Susanne was saying, "—Felicia who called me... and listened."

That was true. Felicia was a listener. Such a flamboyant woman, such a ham, but she listened. She and Salty were a remarkable pair.

Susanne was saying, "—used to take me into their bed—"

"I remember them doing that when I was little."

"What on earth could scare you?" Susanne stopped in mid-gesture for his reply.

"Nightmares."

"The bogeyman?"

"Or variations."

"What made you stay here with me? You could have left. The others were here. You didn't know me from Eve."

"I'd known you for two years—" he began.

"And you'd forgotten me."

"Not really. I'd locked the memory away. I'd felt so sorry for you, then. I didn't know how to help you, but—here—I could."

"You were magnificent. My conscience twinged."

"Only that? You can describe me better than that."

"How?"

He ignored her questioning, and advised, "If you have any brain cells at all, you'll lure me along while you have the chance." And he gave her a bland, lazy look.

"Sampling?"

He licked a smile away. "Not right this minute. You fed me too much."

"Tell me about your travels. Are you finished with that phase of your life? Why did you go? What was it that you wanted?"

He sat back, unaware that she was stroking him. He moved the saltcellar around, as he considered. "I wanted to find an effortless way to make the world better. I'm too impatient with people who don't help themselves. My parents are formidable people. I had to see if I could match them."

"Why just . . . match?"

"For my pride."

" '—that goeth before a fall.' Why confine yourself to their limits? Look at their selfish lives—theatre, cooking and companions to care about."

"Oh, but Susanne, look at the lives they've guided and saved. You. Look at you. You're a fine woman. You were a helpless child. They really care about you." He gestured to the stacks of letters. "You had backing, no matter where you were."

"Felicia wrote about me several times in her family letters. Don't you remember any of the times she told how I was doing?"

"Most of the letters never caught up with me."

"Did you see your picture here on the wall? I have the others, too. I update my share of the wall."

"Do you know how many people they've harbored?" Cray asked. "We were trying to figure it out at Christmastime."

"Full-time, there were seventeen, counting their own five. And then, there were about eight temporaries like me."

"Twenty-five? How do you remember all that? I'd never realized it."

Susanne reminded him, "Then there were the three that Salty supported while he was in the navy. Rod, Michael and John."

"Yeah, I know them. So that makes at least twenty-eight! That's something. And it sure makes a houseful on holidays. You should have seen the mob at Christmas."

"It must have been wonderful."

"Was everyone here for the holidays?" he asked. "Or did they all go home?"

"Petey went to see her folks, but the rest of us were here. It was very nice. We had a tree and gave each other presents. But we had Mrs. Kennedy here and a couple of other neighbors to make the day special."

He said with conviction, "I think I'd like to fool around with you for a while."

"Is this a proposal?"

He considered that as he frowned a little, tilting his head back as he decided. "I don't think so. But it does show that I have a definite interest in you."

"Carnal knowledge," she guessed.

He nodded emphatically. "Definitely."

"You really are a lecher."

"You need to know the real me."

"I'm working on it."

Nine

So the lovers spent the next fifteen hours becoming acquainted in a more intimate way. They exchanged their dreams, their experiences, their hopes for the world. They mostly talked.

Cray gave to Susanne what he hadn't thought to give his family, he told her of his response to the experiences of his travels. He didn't settle down to a droning travelogue, but selected reactions to some of the incidents that had clung to him.

And he told her his observations of manners and mores. He continued to say that although people may seem the same they are not. What they hold precious, changes. What is obvious or friendly to one people is insulting or baffling to another. The God of one is not the God of another. And some gods are adjusted to conform with current beliefs while, in other places, the beliefs force the people to conform.

It was very like the conglomerate of peoples in the United States. Whichever were the beliefs of the vocal majority were the influencing mores or rules.

And sometimes the mores were disguised greed.

At age twenty, to his twenty-six, Susanne was mostly a listener. She had no countering comments, and what he said was something that made sense. To listen to his observations was, for her, a different, stimulating experience. She had never had the time or the leisure to exchange more than party chat.

And he had never had the need to find the listener. It was very satisfying for him to tell his thoughts.

"Did you keep a journal?" she asked.

"No."

"You should write down what you remember. Write the things you've told me. Then go back and write the entire experience of those four years. I'm amazed that Salty didn't see to it that you kept a journal."

"I had four. He sent me one every year. I suppose not writing was a childish part of my rebellion."

She smiled tenderly. "So you recognize it."

He looked off for a while. Then he looked at her. "Only now."

"No, you've known. You told me they are so formidable that you could never match them."

He continued to regard her. Then he said softly, "And you asked why I would limit myself to their accomplishments."

She saw no prejudice in that. No stroking. It was true. "You have such potential. It will be interesting to see how you use your life."

He had a tough time saying the words. "I don't know how to begin."

"You already have. You've begun to see and compare...and judge. I wonder how your yardstick will change."

"For a twenty-year-old, you're very wise."

"You forget that I've been mentally probed and analyzed and advised by a number of therapists. Before I got to Salty and Felicia, I had gone through an avalanche of probing. It was at the beginning of awareness of the extent of sexual abuse in children and the establishment went to overkill. There is no question that the abused child needs help. My own case was far overblown.

"There were some really brilliant, inquisitive minds who gave time to me. And you must remember how susceptible children are to suggestion and how much they want to please 'the teacher,' so that responses can be a problem. I wasn't bothered or abused by my stepfather in the literal sense, I was sexually molested. It wasn't I who needed the emotional help, it was he.

"I have serious reservations about teaching a child 'bad' touching. What happens to a child who is angry with a teacher and that child is coaxed to tell if the teacher did any 'bad' touching? How many children will resist the opportunity to 'punish' the teacher who is disciplining him or her?

"By the time all my own probing and therapy was in full swing, I truly needed help. It was only through the normalness of family love with Salty and Felicia that I survived. I had grown suspicious of all men and some women who had hugged me and tried to give me a feeling of protection. By then, I felt I had been through something horrendous. It was not.''

"Who was the genius who saw what was happening to you?"

"My mother."

"Does she still live here? I've not met her." His voice held curiosity.

"No." Susanne looked down at her hands. "It must have been in one of the letters that didn't find you. My mom died in a car wreck not quite two years ago."

"Well, damn."

"She had really loved my step-dad and grieved to be separated from him. People are so complicated. There are such shadings in character. No one is all good or all bad. We are all so diverse."

"Yeah. It was a tragedy for all of you." They were silent a while before he asked, "After she died, what did you do?"

"I was unsure. Since I had no plans, really, I decided to work awhile and save my money. I found this house, and Sara. Then we interviewed others to join us. We have a safe and secure place. There's good company, comfort and companionship. I suppose they'll all get married and leave me here alone."

"I'll be in the attic," he assured her.

She slid him a sly smile. "Then, if you're there, I'll be there, too."

He drawled lazily, "Got addicted, did you? In just one night? Hot dang! I must be pretty good."

She put back her head to laugh before she gave him a narrow-eyed, tight smile and said, "I hate a bragging man."

He disclaimed that, and corrected her word, "An honest man."

"As I recall, I had to do all the luring. I had to drag you bodily up the stairs, you were so reluctant. You only submitted."

"I'm subtle."

"Then seduce me."

He lounged back and gave her a lazy look. "I don't believe I can rise to the occasion."

She thought that was hilarious.

And he regarded her tenderly. She was so new to sex and men. Actually, she was truly a virgin. Think of all the jokes she hadn't yet heard! And it was he who would tell them to her and watch her laugh.

They got all the week's laundry done and straightened and vacuumed the house. They changed all the beds and hung the washed sheets on the line to blow in the breezes of the Texas day.

They went to the video store and found *The Gods Must be Crazy* and watched it again. That wonderfully amusing film. And they fixed odd foods and sampled and commented.

They enjoyed one another.

And they made love. She instructed him on how to seduce her, and he complied. She said, "You have to compliment me and make me feel beautiful and clever."

He said, "You're beautiful and clever."

"Oh, for Pete's sake! You can do better than that. Be innovative. Be clever and subtle."

He slid over close to her and whispered salaciously about how her body enflamed him and what he wanted to do about it.

She blushed scarlet and gasped. "You have to be more subtle," she scolded.

"Good evening, Miss Taylor, how are you feeling?" And he closed his eyes and put his hands on her intimately.

She wailed, "Cra-aay!"

He opened his eyes and said in surprise, "I was seeing how you're feeling, and I must say I've never felt a better woman in all my li— Of course, I haven't had my hands on any other woman, but if I had, not a one could compare to feeling you."

"You're supposed to tell me my hair is glorious and my eyes are spectacular and my mouth delicious."

He examined those items and said, "Yeah." Then he kissed her the double-whammy kiss she'd declined at breakfast that morning.

After he'd released her and she'd become reoriented, she said, "I've forgotten where we are."

"At your house, in the living room."

She gave him a patient look and explained with labored patience, "In the seduction."

"I just gave you the first kiss."

She smiled a tiny bit. "Yes."

"What's next?" he asked with considerable interest. Then he explained, "I'm rising to the occasion." Then he clarified himself by adding, "To cooperate. In your seduction."

She was in a fit of giggles by then, and he had to simply laugh with her.

"I can't believe some woman hasn't snared you by this time. How have you escaped?"

"I moved around a lot."

"Just 'moseying' along? Loving and leaving?"

"I never saw you along the way, until I finally got to San Antonio."

"How do you like my hair?"

"It's overwashed. You need more of my beard tamer."

She sighed with dramatic patience, but she asked, "And my eyes?"

"Lazy, wicked, filled with humor."

"You're supposed to say like pools of water."

"Dark water." He agreed. "Nighttime. Dangerous."

"Those aren't romantic."

"Mysterious."

"That's a little better." She was patient. Then she prodded, "My lips?"

"Too flat, you need some serious kissing to puff them up and make them red."

"I'll go put on some lipstick."

"Get a flavor I like."

She sat straight and acted a little snippy.

He said, "Come on over here. I know you want to be on my lap, and I just happen to have one available. Come here."

"You can do better than that."

He rose and went to her, then he leaned over and put his hands under her armpits and lifted her, with seeming effortlessness. He held her off the ground and kissed her mouth. Then he arranged her over his shoulder and started for the stairs.

She said, "This isn't comfortable for my stomach."

He stopped, set her briefly on her feet, then picked her up across his arms. He explained, "It would have been easier, the other way, to get you through the doors and up the stairs. This way will be a nuisance, but we can't have your tummy uncomfortable... yet."

"What have you planned, so that my stomach will be uncomfortable?"

"I'm going to lie on it."

"Oh." She curled around him, putting her head on top of his shoulder and wrapping her arms around his shoulders. She curled her knees up so that she was less trouble for him to get through the doors.

That he got her up those stairs without putting her down was an amazing accomplishment. But he did do it, and he made it seem easier than it could have possibly been. He didn't huff or grunt or even swear. And he saw to it that none of her touched a door frame, nor did her head graze the slanted roof of the stairwell. It was a vivid demonstration of his strength.

Men are just stronger than women.

He put her down and stood with an arm holding her close to him as he gestured with the other hand. "This is my version of a cave. You are the prize from my maraudings, and I've brought you here to savor. Strip."

"Just like that?"

He was surprised. "That's what you told me to do yesterday. Have you led me astray? Do I undo buttons?" He crowded her back under the slope of the roof until her head was bent. He rubbed against her in a salacious manner as he searched *everywhere* for her buttons. She had none. But in the search, he left her in a shambles. And in passing, her lips had become puffed and very red.

As he displaced her clothing in his button search, he exposed one breast and exclaimed, "Here's one!" And he twiddled with a reddening nipple. "Hmm." He was stymied. "It doesn't unbutton. How stubborn. It probably needs some lubricant." So he bent his head and earnestly applied the best lubrication immediately available.

With him so diligent, she managed to get his pants undone and opened, and she applied herself with equal concentration. He moved himself in her hands.

She was gasping and her head was wobbly. He was breathing hard through his opened mouth. His face was wickedly amused. Very like a lion's in his sexual roar.

He finished disrobing her, and tore himself out of his own clothing, *and he remembered the condom!* She tried to help him and he became so distracted that he had to stop, so that he could remember what had to be done first.

It was only then that he remembered his bedroll and blanket were out on the clothesline. He put her over his shoulder and carried her down to her own stripped bed. There he had strident basic sex with her, and she was more capable of surviving because the bed was better than the boards, if she had had the time to notice.

When they settled down a little, after having ridden such wild winds of passion, they sighed and patted each other and made contented noises.

She whispered, "I'd never known making love could be so amazing."

"Well, you hadn't met me yet."

She laughed. "Such a modest man."

Quite seriously, he told her, "There's something about you that makes me feel that I'm the only man in the world."

"I think that's so."

"You make me feel that way. You make the most sexual sounds of pleasure and you make such salacious moves, and you have such wicked hands, and you make me feel that there was never a mating to compare to ours."

"I haven't had much experience, this being only the second day, but I believe this is really spectacular. Special."

"Good."

"Let me take off the condom."

"Be careful. I'm a little tender."

"I'll kiss it and make it well."

"You do that and you know what'll happen?"

"What."

"I just thought I ought to warn you."

And he was almost right. But as hot and heavy as they were involved, the thunder did intrude. With the second rumbling, she lifted her head from him and said, "There're clothes on the line!"

—and his bedroll!

They pried themselves up and blindly sought their clothing until they remembered it was in the attic. They staggered up the narrow stairs, jerked on their clothes and ran back downstairs and outside in the first sprinklings. They pitched things into the washhouse and got everything under cover before it could get wet.

And with the downpour, and trapped in the washhouse, he leaned against the wall and said, "It's a great trauma to be pulled from paradise and flung out into a wet storm of the real world."

"We're not in the real world, we've only shifted paradise." Then she showed him how that was. She lay clean towels on the floor, put his sleeping bag on top of that and invited him through the portals.

He had to run through the onslaught of rain to find another condom, but he didn't take very long, and was soon back in her paradise.

Some time later, he said thoughtfully, "You are depleting me."

"Yes. I'm not leaving you any juices that might send you hunting another woman."

"I hadn't thought of that."

"See? It works."

He put his hand in her hair and played with the silken strands. "Even if you didn't 'take my juices,' I wouldn't be looking for another woman. I'd wait for you."

"I could love you, Cray."

"You already do."

"Now, how can you know that?"

"I just know. As you know that I love you. I haven't been able to see another woman since I came here."

"Not until then? I've loved you since I was ten. Half of my life."

"At that time, I was playing basketball and practicing how to walk like a hero. That sort of thing distracts a male."

"I'll have to watch you walk."

"I no longer walk like a hero, because a hero walks like any other man. That way people don't ask him to do too much."

"Do you mean if you walked like a hero, people would ask you to do things?"

"Not just things, but *everything* imaginable. It's too great a chore to be continually plagued to perform miracles. That's why Superman pretends to be Clark Kent."

"Are you being Clark Kent now?"

"I just finished being Superman for you and now I'm in repose."

She bubbled laughter.

He instructed patiently, "One never laughs at a hero, because when she needs one, he won't feel like one and he'll... fail."

"I hadn't known all this."

In repose, he stated, "I know."

As the time passed, and the rainfall continued, they became hungry. They finally folded all the clean clothes and put them in stacks on the dryer, then they rolled his blanket in the tightly rolled sleeping bag, put the floor towels over their heads and ran for the house.

Cray realized the back door had been unlocked the entire time they'd been in the shed. He had Susanne stand by the open back door while he searched the entire house. Everything was in place and okay. He came downstairs, locked the door and kissed her lifted mouth.

They fixed their supper and lazed around, then watched *The Gods Must be Crazy* again.

They went to bed in the attic, and it was so cool that they turned off the air conditioner and opened the opposite window. In the uncharacteristic silence, they kissed in a rather staid manner and . . . slept curled together.

In the morning, he wakened and stealthily raised up on his elbow to look down on his love. She felt the cool air on her naked body and burrowed against him. He smiled, loving it. Loving her.

She wakened, moved to see him watching her and smiled up at him. Then she stretched and yawned. And he got to witness the miracle of that. She was so fascinating.

He ran a slow hand down her amazing body, and she moved like a cat being stroked. He leaned and sipped kisses from her lips. And she turned up her face and puffed her lips to give those to him.

He said, "Good morning, beautiful."

And she said, "I love you, Cray."

"Ahh. That was the perfect reply. Do you want breakfast in bed?"

"I'm not sure if you've noticed, but this sleeping bag is just a medium blanket on bare boards. You have to be enormously impressed that I've spent this entire night with you."

"I'm impressed."

"There were six vacant beds downstairs, and we could have had any two of them."

"I feel like a caveman, and you're my captive."

"You Tarzan—me Jane?"

"Not quite that civilized. And the label yesterday was Superman, if you will recall that."

"Yes, sir."

"Good attitude. You get a kiss."

"Glory be!" The accent was excruciatingly exaggerated.

He kissed her anyway. When he finally lifted his mouth, he mentioned, "It's still raining. Do you recall hearing what is the best thing to do on a rainy day?"

"Let me think. Uhh. Read the Sunday papers?"

"Stay in bed."

"Oh. This can hardly be called a bed. It's only a very small step up from animal skins. But there is merit to the idea."

He ran his hand slowly over her body. "Would you allow me a quickie?"

She looked at him and began to smile a little. "I would allow you anything."

He reached for the condom, and she watched him put it on. He turned to her, and she welcomed him, rather amused.

He was serious. He kissed her ardently. His hands worked her, and he allowed his passion instantly full rein, no holds barred, no restraint, no hesitation, full-out and wild. He took her, and his ride was swift and wild. He thundered to a halt and collapsed on her, his heart galloping, his breathing harsh, his body limp as a wet rag.

She put her arms around him and held him in bemusement.

He began to separate from her. He kissed her cheek and said, "Thank you for that."

"How astonishing."

"Why?" He was sitting up and turned back toward her. He was magnificently naked and male.

"I've heard of the wam-bam-thank you, ma'am, but I had no idea how accurate it was."

"If you feel left out, I can take care of that."

"Not right now. I'm just amazed it took such a short time. It must be maddening for you to take as long as I like."

"Taking a long time is just as great as a quickie. But doing it this way is also great. I appreciate you holding still for it."

"I really didn't have time to react."

He grinned and waggled her head, then he leaned over and kissed her sweetly. "You are a gem."

"And I'm expensive, I like to eat."

"Rats. I knew there was a flaw in you. There had to be! So you eat."

"You fixed my breakfast yesterday, I'll do yours today."

"Fair enough. What?"

"I'm pretty good at French toast."

"I'll accept French toast."

"I'll go shower, and I'll call you when I'm through."

She stretched and made murmuring sounds. He hunkered down and watched her. "You've made a lucky escape by giving me my way a while ago."

"I'll get you later."

"I'll look forward to it." He stretched along her on hands and one knee, and he kissed her.

It was excessively male and primitive. How could that be? It was probably his talk about the attic being his cave that brought that to her mind. But he was really a very basic man.

Even the fact that he coddled her was basic. She gave him release, and he spoiled her in gratitude. It was the way of men. If these were really cave days, he would bring her a necklace of bear claws and knuckle-bones.

And the thought of how a man got knuckle bones was sobering. She thought of times when people lived by their wits and in small groups and defended themselves. Cray would survive. He would fill her with babies, and he would defend them and keep them safe. And in these times, he would do the modern version of that. He would care for her and keep her safe.

"Shower's ready," he called up the stairs.

Bemused, Susanne rolled up and continued to think of Cray. She went naked down the stairs and into her room where she chose just a dress to wear. She expected to make love with him, and she knew the dress was thin enough to entice his glances, his stares. She smiled.

She stood under the warm water and slowly soaped her body, rinsing herself in the warm water.

She dried her hair, put on some eye makeup and considered herself. She smiled at her reflection. Life was good. Cray was a miracle.

She went barefoot out to the kitchen, and Cray was ready to fry the French toast.

She drank the juice he offered and rewarded him with a sweet kiss. She saw him look down her and saw that he smiled just a little, but he didn't comment on the fact that the dress was fairly transparent.

He watched her through breakfast, and she finally asked, "Is there something wrong with my dress?"

And she made her questioning expression mildly interested in his reply.

He chewed and swallowed as she waited, and then he replied, "I'm trying to think of a way to keep you warm without putting any more clothing on you."

And she laughed.

They made church by the skin of their teeth and they did hear the sermon. She wore different clothing. They were admonished about "loving thy fellow man." They were staunch enough not to exchange a glance.

They went out for dinner at the buffet at the mall out past Alamo Heights on Broadway. Susanne ate an acceptable amount, but Cray stuffed himself. When she commented on that, Cray explained, "I had only a little French toast for breakfast."

They spent the afternoon in the attic, dozing and making love and anguishing over the return of the housemates.

"We'll find our own house," he told her.

"But I'd miss seeing them all."

"Move up here."

"That would be a scandal."

"You could marry me."

"What a good idea!"

"How can you act so surprised, when you've led me right to it?"

"Oh, did you notice that?"

"I've known all along what you intended."

"When?"

"When you let me give you those double-whammy kisses that first day."

"You knew *then*?"

"Yep."

"Have you noticed how many western expressions you're picking up?"

"I've been here a couple of months and I'm acclimatized."

"You plan to stay?"

"I like the weather."

"Cray, it's raining!"

"Now that I'm a Texan, I know how precious rain can be."

"Good grief."

Ten

The housemates arrived in a flurry of excitement and greetings and a whole lot of chatter. Cray had forgotten what a noisy bunch they were and how amazingly quiet the house had been with them all gone.

"Did you behave?" Sharon asked Susanne, with a smug little smile.

Cray wasn't sure how Susanne would respond, and he didn't want her hagridden. He felt the stirrings of protectiveness growing inside his heart. He opened his mo—

"Perfectly." Susanne replied placidly.

He gave her a slight smile of pride and asked a less personal question. "How was the Heavy Weather group?"

"As good live as they are on a careful tape. It was such a wonderful evening. What musicians! You all should have gone."

Cray replied kindly, "Who would have cleaned the house and caught up on all the laundry?"

And surprisingly it was Petey who exclaimed, "When did you all have time to do that?"

The women laughed. Then one inquired in a purr, "How was the picnic, Susanne?"

She walked over to Cray and put her arms around one of his as she leaned against him. With some sly smugness, she explained, "I called in and said I had to spend the weekend in bed."

Cray laughed with the rest, and he watched Susanne's laughing eyes and smug blush. The cat was out of the bag.

So Susanne slept in the attic that night.

When it was clear to the other five that Susanne was going to sleep with Cray in the attic, there had been a spirited debate on which bedroom would give up a bed. A good try was made to select one of the remaining five to take the studio couch, maybe by drawing straws? That didn't win any votes. The lure was that then each bedroom would have only two beds. While the whole deal fell through, the try was decidedly loud, quite hilarious and not at all serious.

Of course, as soon as the pair had gone up the attic stairs, there was broom-handle pounding on the ceilings below with shouts of, "Cut that out! We have to get some sleep."

And in the attic, Cray mentioned to Susanne, "You *told* them."

"Was it a secret?"

"It's a good thing I was already committed, or I'd find myself with five shotguns shoved up my rear."

"They're more subtle."

With the renewed pounding, Cray questioned, "That's...subtle?"

"That's humor."

With the weekend having been as physical as it was, the lovers kissed good-night in sweet murmurings and sighed themselves into sleep. And they slept solidly, flat out.

The rested lovers had to laugh at the sly innuendos the next morning. They even scoffed. But the smug exchange of knowing glances couldn't be allayed. Petey complained, "I stayed awake all night, listening, trying to hear what you were doing. I'm exhausted." And the others agreed, faking yawns and complaining.

The lovers kissed goodbye before them all. It was a brief, unbody-touching salute, but the women carried on as if Rudolph Valentino's ghost had slipped into Cray's body.

As usual, they all went off in all directions, and the day began.

For Cray, it was a long, long day. Everybody in San Antonio had rented a car or ruined a taxi. Then, there were those independent citizens who demanded the same immediate service, and Pepper's Auto Service and Repair was chaos. Actually, it was a normal Monday, the alleged chaos was Cray's attitude. He wanted to be back with Susanne, and time dragged excruciatingly.

Quitting time finally came. Cray went home and, as was usual, the three cars were lined up in the drive. But there was no sign of anyone. He parked in front of the house, got out, and pondered the reason for the prickle up his spine. The shades were drawn in the living room. He went up the walk and onto the porch. He saw with some sobered attention that the bedroom shades had been drawn and the door was closed.

What instinct tipped him off? He didn't use his key, he knocked. No one came in response.

He stood a minute, then went down the porch steps and along the drive around to the back. All the shades were pulled, the house was silent and no one was out in the washhouse. Even with his car at the curb and his footsteps down the driveway, Susanne hadn't come to the door.

It was too strange that she did not. She could not? And if she wasn't yet home, wouldn't one of the other women have opened the door?

Or was this a surprise party?

It would be too early, too quick.

There was something . . . wrong.

He went back to his car and drove away. He went to the closest public phone and called Susanne. There was no answer. With three cars in the driveway, there had to be someone at the house.

Cray dialed again—very carefully, to be sure he'd dialed right—and he let it ring. Then he called the police station, gave his name and his location and asked for Bart Collins. He told the police sergeant exactly why he was calling and asked that Collins return the call to that phone booth immediately.

In a miracle, Bart called him a little over five minutes later, sleepily, from his house.

Cray began, "This could be a false alarm. I can't take the chance." And he told Bart what had happened, that it could be a surprise party, but no one had answered the phone at the house. "You know about the sharks. There are six women in there. One is Susanne. I *have* to get back—now—and try to get inside."

"Stay where you are."

"I can't."

"I'll be there in ten minutes."

"They could already be dead by then."

"Wait. Wait right there, or it could be you. Don't go back. Wait. This is a police order."

"Listen to me. Not everyone knows about the attic. All the shades are down. You might be able to sneak in from the garage roof by ladder in the back. From the attic, you come down a solid stair into the back bedroom. I'll be a diversion. I'll see you there." And Cray hung up with Bart yelling, "No!"

Cray drove back to the house. He passed two unmarked cars, each with two men inside. He avoided their delaying signals and pulled up again in front of the little house. It was as it had been—the shades were drawn on all the windows and the house still.

Down the street, men left the unmarked cars and melted away, screened by the houses. They were police? They'd gotten there already? Impossible.

He heard cars on the street, on through behind the house. That was probably just ordinary after-work traffic to the apartment rabbit warren on the hill.

His skin prickled, for he knew that Susanne was inside the house. He went to the front door and the screen was locked. It was an old-fashioned wooden frame with a hook holding the door.

With his pocket knife, he slit the screen as a car cruised past. He unlatched the screen and opened it.

He inserted his key and opened the door calling, "I'm home!"

And he saw petrified women, a starkly staring Susanne, and a man.

With credible cool, he asked, "Company?"

The man was nervous and hesitated.

Cray seemed so relaxed, so interested in a kind of way.

The man said, "Get—"

Cray said in an apologetic manner, "That one's a firecracker, she's a real hellcat. She'd de-sex you in a minute. Even in these circumstances, she'll blow." And he nodded, agreeing with his words.

Cray was being a distraction. He had the guy's attenti— And another man came from the back of the house. He had a gun.

"Well," Cray said brightly, "two of you? How did you get inside? I've told them to lock their doors. Steady, honey, now isn't the time for any heroineics." He looked at the cowardly Petey, after a fleeting look at the steady Sharon.

There was the slightest, barest sound in the attic. A mouse? Or had the rescuers arrived? This soon? No way. It was the result of the desperation of his wishful thinking.

The first man snarled. "You made a big mistake, coming inside."

"In what way?" He'd gradually moved enough so that—in that small room—he could get a hand on Susanne.

"You're dead meat." The gun holder actually did say that.

Cray chided logically, "That would be foolish. Picking up girls is one thing, but an out-and-out killing is frowned on. You have to know that."

"Shut up."

Cray looked beyond them into the kitchen and said, "Well, hello!"

And just about all of them turned to look, as Cray pulled Susanne behind him and backed swiftly to the door in a stumbling, scrambling move to thrust her onto the porch as the gun went off.

Cray shouted and all the women screamed at the tops of their lungs, Sharon hit one of the men with something and bedlam ensued!

Cray staggered back against the door and began to slide down. Men erupted into the kitchen and through the front door and it was all over. Mostly.

The screaming was echoed outside. It was Susanne. Cray knew that. Against the open front door, he was slowly sliding to the floor, resisting his body's surrender. His sight was going, his ears still hearing one close-by case of impressive hysteria before oblivion overtook him. He was dying? Dead? He felt great regret as he lost everything and dark silence enveloped him.

Such a small house was easy to shake down for any other intruders. Everyone talked at once, and the police were kind enough to allow that first edge of pent-up hysteria to be given voice. Their own voices were calming, and two of them gave quick attention to the still figure by the front door.

Susanne had torn herself from the plainclothesman outside and was trying to get to Cray. There was opposition. Sharon had to tell them to release her, that the woman was one of them, she had been inside. Cray had thrown Susanne outside. Cray was the man on the floor by the front door.

The swarming police allowed Susanne inside, but she couldn't get close to Cray. She was wringing her hands and crying. Two men were working on Cray. He was alive. He'd been shot in the shoulder and inside his right thigh. He was still unconscious. They were trying to stem the flow of blood.

The other man on the floor was still out cold from the blow Sharon had dealt. She was still ready to wallop just about anyone and finally slapped the hysterical Trish.

A reasonable silence descended.

Outside there were TV camera people, microphones attached to pushy people, neighbors, passersby, and people who stared and questioned. Mrs. Kennedy volunteered information and gave all sorts of replies.

The ambulance came edging through, its lights flashing; the police were shouting, trying to help with the progress of the vehicle through the pressing spectators.

Cray was carried out finally, and Susanne was with him. He was very pale, but still looked handsome under the circumstances, and he made a great visual for TV. And Susanne was gorgeously distracted and dismayed and controlled. She was totally unaware of anything but Cray, and the cameras followed her avidly. She made terrific drama.

The sullen first man and the second man, who had been revived from Sharon's blow, were taken out of the house and put into police cars. The TV lights were very bright. And the first man snarled at them. It was great for the camera.

The reporters relayed requests for interviews, but were declined. So they interviewed Mrs. Kennedy. That's how history is concocted.

The residue of police questioning and examination and tidying and evidence finding took a while.

None of the housemates wanted supper. Ellen made coffee, and that was a mistake for it made them all more hyper, but the police appreciated it. Their veins were laminated with caffeine.

The terrible time was over. It seemed, then, to be unreal. The housemates couldn't believe it had even happened. They were anxious about Cray. Ellen and Sara went to the hospital to find Susanne and stay with her.

Salty came down to check on his wounded child. And he observed Susanne who was also under his concern. He surveyed the house, and he slept in the attic. He went to the hospital and sat by Cray.

When Cray became cognizant, he was almost as pale as the white sheets on his hospital bed, and he was connected to tubes and a blood transfusion. One of his hands was permanently connected to Susanne. He told his dad, "I could have used you for a while there."

Salty had to clear his raspy throat. "Who you want me to bend?"

"There's no need, now. The San Antonio police department substituted for you."

Salty could laugh, then. "You comparing me to the city's whole police department?"

"I was taught that respect as a very small child."

"God, Cray—" his father's voice was especially roughened "—you scared us."

"I scared me pretty good, too, but Susanne was in that house."

"I know the feeling."

"You didn't have to come down. You knew I was all right. Felicia will miss you."

"We talk on the phone. Bob and Jo are there. Do the wounds hurt bad?"

"They've got me doped a little and everything is euphoric—or maybe I'm just amazed I'm still alive."

"Thank God for that."

"Did you hear where I was shot?"

"Your shoulder and—"

"The shoulder is a normal place, but that bastard shot me on the inside of my right thigh, high up! Close. My God, Dad, I could have been ruined!"

"But you weren't."

"I guess it's obvious God intends me to help replenish the species."

"Oh-oh. Hear that Susanne? You'd better get the preacher up here right away."

Salty didn't stay long before he had to get back home. "Come up when you can," he urged Cray and Susanne. "Everyone will be anxious to see you."

"We'll send them a videotape. You going to stop and see Pepper?"

"Yeah. He was here while you were still out of it. He thought you might be faking it, so that he'd have to run the business again himself."

"Run the business?" Susanne was tasting the words.

"Yeah," said Salty. "At Pepper's auto-repair business."

"Cray... runs it?"

"Didn't he tell you?"

Cray sighed. "My head hurts."

Susanne scoffed, "It wasn't your head that was hit, yet. Do you know he's been living in our attic because he had no money?"

"He's my son, all right."

"Why, Salty!"

And Salty laughed in raspy puffs.

The ramifications of the disruption festered inside the housemates, making them jumpy and afraid. They were offered help from the city stress-counselling service, and they took advantage of it. With practiced skill, the counselors helped them put the experience into perspective.

Bart Collins, the policeman, came by to check on the five left at the house over the next week, and he became ensnared by Petey. He would say, "If you weren't still afraid of the sharks, would you be dating me?"

And she would tilt back her head and reply, "Probably not."

That frustrated the living hell out of him.

And when Susanne brought Cray home to the crowded little house, the five women and Bart were all there, having taken the day off. Cray wobbled inside, favoring the fragile right leg, and the women were stricken that their hero had suffered.

Bart advised in an aside, "Milk it while you got it."

They all took Cray to the attic where a great double bed took up almost a fourth of the attic. Cray just laughed.

When he could speak, he inquired avidly, "How in *hell* did you get it up here?"

And they all told him. They put their hands to their heads and shook their heads and waved their arms, and finally Bart said, "They lifted the roof and dropped it in."

That had to've been the only way it could have been done.

The air conditioner had been moved over and set into the wall, freeing that front window. With the air cool in the April day, the windows had been carefully washed and left open. His new nest was really cozy.

He went to bed, depleted by the trip home. He lay there, covered by the light blanket, and he smiled at the people crowded in that hampered space.

"Tell me," he urged. "How did those guys get inside? Susanne never told me."

"Trish went out to the washhouse and left the back door open. It wasn't careless, we were all here. The first guy sneaked in, sometime during that time. She came back and the second guy came in right after her."

Sharon added, "We weren't terribly alarmed. There were six of us and only two of them. Men are stronger. When they don't care about women, they can easily hurt them."

They had been hurt? Cray wasn't ready to hear that until he was stronger.

Petey said, "We didn't worry, because we knew you would be there soon. But you came to the door and knocked. We've been so curious as to why you knocked?''

"Yes. What tipped you off?"

"I'm not sure. You all are never that quiet. And the shades in the living room had been drawn. That wasn't usual. Then, when I called, no one answered the phone. With three cars in the drive, I knew you had to be here. I called Bart."

"I gave him a police order not to come back alone. He hung up on me."

"I thought they'd killed you." Agnes' voice wavered.

Cray took a deep, careful breath and said, "I thought so, too."

Susanne gave a watery sound of distress.

"I'm fine." Cray reached his hand for hers, and she crawled up the bed to sit beside him under the slanting roof.

"When you bullied your way inside, using your key, the other man stayed out of your sight. He said he'd kill us if we said a word. We didn't know what to do."

Cray said in a roughened voice, "They weren't there to rob you."

"That, too."

"Were any of you harmed?"

"They were about to begin when you came by the first time. That rattled them. Then you came back. We didn't mention that you could get inside. We thought when you opened the door, we'd jump them. Sara and I had communicated that, and we knew the rest would react immediately. It was only then we found out the one had a gun."

"That would tend to make you hesitate."

"You were magnificent." Agnes was earnest.

They all made ardent murmurs, agreeing. "You were our hope." That was Sharon. "We have no idea you'd been smart enough to alert the police."

Cray grinned at that backhanded compliment.

"Police prefer to be alerted ahead of time." Bart put that in. "They always hope it's a false alarm. But it's better to call and have someone know what might be going on, than to try to solve something alone. It upsets us to get there after the fact. We about went crazy getting there in time to save your necks. Cray should'a waited for us. It makes us mad to have to mop up some dumb fool who thinks he's Superman."

That hit a chord in Susanne. Cray had said he was Superman. She looked down at him. He was "in repose," pale and wan.

Ellen said softly, "Coming home must have exhausted Cray. We ought to let him rest."

Cray quirked his lips tiredly. He allowed his eyelids to appear heavy.

They all told him variations about getting his rest and taking care of himself, and they trailed down the stairs and were surprisingly quiet.

"Do you want anything?"

"How in hell did they get this bed up here?"

"Aren't you touched that they'd do that? It must have been an awful job. It *is* twin beds that have been strapped together. As I understand it, they removed that window in the back and brought everything in through there. Did you notice we have a toilet sitting there in the middle of the floor?"

Laughter tickled through Cray and he said, "It was obvious. And it was very kind. We can't stay here. It's too crowded, as it is."

"We'll have to stay for a while. With all this effort, we can't *not* stay. We have to allow them to do this."

Cray looked at his love. "Tell me that you love me."

"Oh, Cray. When I heard those shots, I knew they'd hit you. You came in there just as if you were immortal. You terrified me. I didn't know what to do to protect you from your stupidity."

"Stupidity?"

"Coming barreling into a house under siege. Why didn't you wait for the police?"

"I didn't know what was happening to you. I knew you were in the house, but there were no sounds. I didn't know if you were already dead."

"My God, Cray. When I realized you were going to come into the house, I tried to think of a way to warn you without jeopardizing the others. I was frantic!"

"You all appeared remarkably calm. I was impressed."

"It was a false impression. I knew that Sharon was plotting. She would. I was waiting for a signal from her, to do whatever she indicated."

"Once there were nine nurses in Chicago who were captured in a group by one man. He killed them one by one. They went past the time when the full group could have attacked him together and most of them would have won. They all lost."

"We were almost beyond that point."

"Yes."

"I'm glad you lived."

"I am, too. When I was losing consciousness, I thought I was dying. I couldn't control my lucidity and I thought I'd lost."

"You would have given your life for me. I couldn't have lived it without you."

"Yes, you could."

"I remember thinking of you as a man of another time, who would protect his family against all odds. That comforted me until I saw that you would still do it, in these times, against real danger. I didn't know what to do to stop you."

"I love you, Susanne."

"I love you, Cray. Will you please take better care of yourself?"

"Yes. Kiss me sweetly and lie against my side so that I can know you're really here with me."

She did that. The breeze came through the front window and went on out the back one. They both slept.

One of the girls came up the stairs and knocked a couple of times, then peeked. She came to them and spread a cover over Susanne, then she left them there, setting a jug of hot bouillon on a little table.

It was quiet. The people downstairs tiptoed around in stocking feet and whispered.

It was suppertime when Susanne wakened. She stirred and looked soberly at her sleeping love. Her heart squeezed with the pain of love and she felt a tear roll down her cheek.

He slept so hard that she could ease away from him and leave the bed.

They wakened him for supper. They'd cut a cardboard box so that it was a sturdy wedge. That way it was a backrest under his pillow so that he could sit up to eat.

And he slept that night with Susanne by his side.

By the evening of the next day, Cray was up. The women all fluttered, and Bart helped him down the stairs. Bart complained, "I always felt lucky not to be shot, but I can see advanta—"

Petey interrupted, "Don't even *say* it!" She was strident and angry.

Bart grinned ear-to-ear, having never before known that a strident, angry woman could melt a man's heart.

Cray sat down at the table and he was served. Susanne was not one of the servers. She sat next to Cray and held his left hand. He ate with his right one.

He didn't say much. They all talked at him. They were simply charming. He looked at Susanne and said, "Do you realize they will be our family all the rest of our lives?"

She nodded.

And later, as they lay on the new bed in the attic, Cray said to Susanne, "I think I'd better ask you, right now, how many children you intend to have."

"That would be open to negotiation."

"Quick." He nodded. "You knew I'd want to know?"

"I wasn't sure you would agree to almost thirty children, the way of your parents."

He put his hand on his chest and gasped. "Thirty?"

"Well, you wouldn't have to give them all to me. We could take in some kids."

"I don't have Salty's nest egg to support and feed that many mouths."

"You could get a job."

"I do have one. I'm supervisor and top muckity-muck for Pepper. He pays me quite well. But not enough for—gasp—thirty kids."

"Well, I did say that was negotiable."

"How are you going to go about your side of the negotiations?"

"I thought I'd start later, after we're married."

"You could . . . practice."

"Are you healthy enough?"

"Willing."

And he certainly was.

They were married that summer in Temple, Ohio, at the Browns' house. Everyone was there, including the Texas additions to the family.

At one point, in all the noise, Cray asked Susanne, "Doesn't this mob make you a little more thoughtful when it comes to kids?"

She grinned widely and then laughed.

*   *   *   *   *

SILHOUETTE® Desire™

COMING NEXT MONTH

#733 THE CASE OF THE MISSING SECRETARY—Diana Palmer
MOST WANTED
Logan Deverell disliked disruption of his orderly life. But when
secretary Kit Morris decided this bear had been left in hibernation too
long, suddenly calm turned to chaos!

#734 LOVE TEXAS STYLE!—Annette Broadrick
SONS OF TEXAS
Allison Alvarez didn't need any help raising her son, especially not
from rugged businessman Cole Callaway—the man who had turned
his back on her and her baby fifteen long years ago....

#735 DOUBLECROSS—Mary Maxwell
Secret agent Travis Cross was hunting a murderer. But while hiding
out with sexy schoolteacher Alexis Wright, he caught a case of the
chicken pox, and the prescription was love!

#736 HELD HOSTAGE—Jean Barrett
When timid Regan MacLeod was stranded in the snowy wilderness
with accused murderer Adam Fuller, she knew survival depended on
trusting the handsome, bitter man—that and body heat....

#737 UNTOUCHED BY MAN—Laura Leone
As far as scholarly Clowance Masterson was concerned,
Michael O'Grady was a disreputable swindler. But the more time they
spent together, the more she fell prey to his seductive charm....

#738 NAVARRONE—Helen R. Myers
September's *Man of the Month*, Navarrone Santee, had only one
priority—proving his longtime enemy was a brutal killer. But his
efforts were blocked by sultry Dr. Erin Hayes.

AVAILABLE NOW:

Take 4 bestselling love stories FREE

Plus get a FREE surprise gift!